W9-BHS-642

"What don't you want me to do, Romi, my sweet virgin?" Why did those words sound so hot in Max's voice? *"Turn you on? You weren't complaining a second ago."*

She couldn't deny it. Wasn't sure she wanted to, even if she could. "Neither were you."

But he'd stopped and she hadn't even thought to try. Darn him.

"No, and I never will."

Why did he have to say things like that? Things that could make her hope when hope and this man did not go together. "We still want different things."

"Are you so sure? If I hadn't stopped, you would have let me take you here and now."

He was talking about sex when she was referring to a relationship. And he knew it. "Do you get some thrill out of reminding me of my own weakness?"

"It's not a weakness, *milaya*."

Lucy Monroe's

Ruthless Russians

Passion is in their blood

As boys, they came from Russia to America to make their fortunes. Now formidable opponents in the boardroom, Viktor Beck and Maxwell Black are about to make the biggest acquisitions of their lives by marrying two of San Francisco's most notorious heiresses! Beneath their suave American exteriors beat the passionate hearts of fearsome Cossack warriors—and their intended brides are about to give them the battle of their lives!

An Heiress for His Empire

A tabloid sex scandal means Viktor Beck can put his plan in motion and marry heiress Madison Archer— the key to taking over her father's business and building his empire. But even this ruthless Russian is not prepared for his wild bride to be a virgin!

October 2014

A Virgin for His Prize

Formidable CEO Maxwell Black is about to make his ultimate acquisition—socialite Romi Grayson! She has something he wants, and his need for control—in all areas—means he won't rest until his ring is on her finger...and the innocent Romi is warm and willing in his bed!

November 2014

Lucy Monroe

—

A Virgin for His Prize

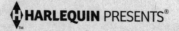

HARLEQUIN PRESENTS®

If you purchased this book without a cover you should be aware that this book is stolen property. It was reported as "unsold and destroyed" to the publisher, and neither the author nor the publisher has received any payment for this "stripped book."

Recycling programs
for this product may
not exist in your area.

ISBN-13: 978-0-373-13288-1

A Virgin for His Prize

First North American Publication 2014

Copyright © 2014 by Lucy Monroe

All rights reserved. Except for use in any review, the reproduction or utilization of this work in whole or in part in any form by any electronic, mechanical or other means, now known or hereinafter invented, including xerography, photocopying and recording, or in any information storage or retrieval system, is forbidden without the written permission of the publisher, Harlequin Enterprises Limited, 225 Duncan Mill Road, Don Mills, Ontario M3B 3K9, Canada.

This is a work of fiction. Names, characters, places and incidents are either the product of the author's imagination or are used fictitiously, and any resemblance to actual persons, living or dead, business establishments, events or locales is entirely coincidental.

This edition published by arrangement with Harlequin Books S.A.

For questions and comments about the quality of this book, please contact us at CustomerService@Harlequin.com.

® and TM are trademarks of Harlequin Enterprises Limited or its corporate affiliates. Trademarks indicated with ® are registered in the United States Patent and Trademark Office, the Canadian Intellectual Property Office and in other countries.

Printed in U.S.A.

www.Harlequin.com

All about the author...
Lucy Monroe

Award-winning and bestselling author **LUCY MONROE** sold her first book in September 2002 to the Harlequin Presents® line. That book represented a dream that had been burning in her heart for years—the dream to share her stories with readers who love romance as much as she does. Since then she has sold more than thirty books to three publishers and hit national bestsellers lists in the U.S. and England, but what has touched her most deeply since selling that first book are the reader letters she receives. Her most important goal with every book is to touch a reader's heart, and when she hears she's done that it makes every night spent writing into the wee hours of morning worth it.

She started reading Harlequin Presents® books when she was very young and discovered a heroic type of man between the covers of those books...an honorable man, capable of faithfulness and sacrifice for the people he loves. Now married to what she terms her "alpha male at the end of a book," Lucy believes there is a lot more reality to the fantasy stories she writes than most people give credit for. She believes in happy endings that are really marvelous beginnings, and that's why she writes them. She hopes her books help readers to believe a little, too...just as romance did for her so many years ago.

She really does love to hear from readers and responds to every email. You can reach her by emailing lucymonroe@lucymonroe.com.

Other titles by Lucy Monroe available in ebook:

SHEIKH'S SCANDAL (*The Chatsfield*)
MILLION DOLLAR CHRISTMAS PROPOSAL
PRINCE OF SECRETS (*By His Royal Decree*)
ONE NIGHT HEIR (*By His Royal Decree*)

In honor of The Gathering Place and the two amazing families who have created this wonderful sanctuary they so generously share with those blessed enough to call them both friend and family. I have never written a book in a more peaceful and love-filled environment.
Thank you!

CHAPTER ONE

FURY FIGHTING WITH the pain of betrayal, Romi Grayson set her phone down on the table beside her with careful movements. The temptation to throw the mobile device across the room was staggering.

That lying, manipulative, opportunistic *tycoon!*

Maxwell Black had made it very clear to Romi that he wasn't in the market for a long-term relationship, but that hadn't meant he wasn't interested in something else. His generosity in and out of bed with his lovers had been the fodder for gossip for years. As were the unexpectedly amicable breakups.

Max had promised Romi sexual pleasure beyond the scope of her imagination.

He'd said she would be the sole focus of his interest.

Until he was done with her.

The *über*-wealthy tycoon-playboy had offered Romi absolute fidelity *with a time limit*.

She'd walked away.

From the promise. From the possibilities. From the certainty of a broken heart.

They'd only dated a few times, but he'd sparked a depth of emotion in her that was both immediate and frightening. Terrifying for its intensity, Romi had had no doubts that she wouldn't survive a breakup down the road with her heart intact.

Walking away after their short, almost platonic association had been painful enough. *Almost* being the operative word. Max had given Romi her first taste of sexual pleasure with a partner.

Awed by the sensations he evoked, she'd been close to giving in to Max's offer.

Ultimately, she'd had no choice, though. Not with his attitude.

For all her "free-spirited" ways, Romi was a traditionalist at heart. She wanted a home, a family and the man she loved to be looking at the future, not the expiry date on their relationship.

That same man had been prepared to *marry* Romi's sister-by-choice, Madison Archer.

For a payoff!

Shares in Archer International Holdings and the prospect of taking over when Jeremy Archer retired had tempted Maxwell Black to break his "no commitments" rule.

The mercenary *cad*.

It was an old-fashioned word, but man, it *fit*.

"Ramona!" Her dad's wavering call came from the den he spent most of his time in these days.

He only made it into the office about two days a week, his longtime director of operations running Grayson Enterprises in everything but name.

Some might have expected Romi to take over the family business, but not her dad. Harry Grayson had always made it clear he expected his daughter to follow her own dreams.

Filtered sunlight from the single window on the north side cast the den in gray light. Her father sat on the sofa facing the dark screen of a wall-mounted big-screen television. The highball glass in his hand was empty but for a couple of ice cubes. Bloodshot, red-rimmed hazel eyes testified to the fact it hadn't been empty for long, or often in the past hours.

She walked forward and took the glass from his unresisting fingers. "It's only afternoon, Daddy. You don't need this."

There was a time when he hadn't picked up a drink with alcohol in it before the cocktail hour. He'd drunk steadily from that point so that he went to bed every night so inebriated, walking up the stairs was a danger.

But the drinking hadn't gone on during the day.

Over the past few years, the drinking had gotten worse while she was away at school. Her father now started at lunchtime with a glass of wine that often became a bottle.

But drinking hard liquor this early in the day was still something new.

Recognition took seconds to register in his rheumy gaze. "Ramona."

"Yes, Daddy. You called me." Something he never would have done sober.

Graysons did not do *common* things like shout through the house for one another. They used the intercom system.

But Harry Grayson didn't look in any shape to cross the room to the intercom. His brows drew together in an exaggerated effort at concentrating. "I did?"

"Yes, Daddy, you did."

He looked with confusion around the room, like the answer might leap out at him. "I think I lost the remote."

Romi bent down and picked up the small electronic device from the floor at his feet. "Here it is."

"Oh, thank you." He frowned. "It's not working."

She swiped her hand on the screen and spoke the command to turn the TV on. The sound of afternoon news commentary filled the room from the surround-sound speakers.

"It's working just fine."

"Wouldn't turn on for me," her father slurred.

She wasn't surprised. The remote was programmed to take voice instruction with recognizable commands, not speech blurred by alcohol.

"You look upset, kitten."

That was the thing about her dad. Even with his brain pickled by too much drink, he cared about her. He paid attention. She had no trouble remembering that even drunk, her dad was twice the father than a man like Maddie's dad could ever hope to be.

"I'm okay."

"No, you're not." He was careful to enunciate every word.

And for some reason that made Romi feel like crying. "It's nothing, really."

"No, I know it's something." For just a moment, her dad wasn't a drunk bent on destroying his liver.

He was the man who had loved her mother so much, he'd married her against his own family's wishes. He was the guy who raised Romi from the time she was three, refusing the easy road of allowing other family members to take on her care.

"It's an old story." And she'd fallen for it.

"Tell me."

"I fell for a man."

"You didn't tell me."

Romi ignored that, incapable of coming up with a response that wouldn't hurt one of them. "He told me he didn't do commitment."

"And you found out he's married?" her dad asked, looking as angry as emotions dulled by overimbibing would allow.

"No, but I did find out he's willing to get married. For the right price."

"The cad!"

She couldn't help smiling at how her father's word echoed her own thoughts just a few minutes before. "Exactly."

"You're better off without him."

"Of course." If only she could convince her heart as easily as her head.

Maxwell Black was bored. Attending these functions rarely provided anything but a few mind-numbing hours interspersed with brief moments of useful networking.

Oh, he believed in the cause. Tonight's gala was dedicated to raising funds for and awareness of the plight of hunger among school-age children.

Considering the focus of the evening, he might have an opportunity to indulge in one of his favorite pastimes. Watching Romi Grayson.

Touching her was more satisfying, but she'd turned down his offer of a liaison in no uncertain terms.

In a rare show of restraint, he hadn't continued the pursuit.

There was something different...almost *special*...about the old-money San Francisco heiress, a vulnerability he was unwilling to exploit.

A first for him—he'd stayed away from her as much out of self-preservation as anything else.

He felt protective toward her in ways he did not understand, ways that could be manipulated if she knew about them. So, she would never find out.

Even so, plans and intentions changed and he was coming to the conclusion that he and Romi might have a future after all. So long as Maxwell dictated the terms.

The soft scent of jasmine and vanilla he always associated with the heiress activist reached him before she did.

"Well, well, well, if it isn't Maxwell Black, *master* tycoon."

Squelching the urge to turn quickly, he slowly faced her.

Black, silky chin-length hair framed Romi's pixie-like features, her bow-shaped lips set in an uncustomary flat line. Her makeup was dramatic tonight, bringing out the gentian blue of her eyes. Eyes that snapped with accusation he did not understand.

Or perhaps he did.

"Good evening, Romi. You look lovely tonight."

The elegant peacock-blue evening gown accented her modest curves, highlighting Romi's particular brand of delicate femininity. Fragility at odds with her gung-ho approach to life. Romi didn't consider any cause too great, or any opponent too intimidating to take on.

Borderline petite at five foot five, with a personality that more than made up for her smaller stature, Maxwell had found Ramona Grayson intriguing from their first meeting.

"Thank you." She frowned at him, but offered grudgingly, "You're very handsome yourself tonight. Not a designer I recognize. A tuxedo from one of the tailors on Savile Row?"

He smiled, impressed by her powers of observation. Having his clothing made to fit could be considered a luxury by some, but for Maxwell it was more than that. Tailored designer brands impressed, but having a *bespoke* suit, patterned and constructed entirely to his specifications, made another kind of impression, one in line with Maxwell's reputation for utter control in and out of the boardroom.

"My suit-maker is local, but he apprenticed with a Savile Row tailor."

"Of course. I notice you don't give his name."

"Why? Are you looking for a new tailor for your father?" Not that Maxwell thought his would take on Grayson.

The tailor was both expensive and extremely discerning about his clientele. An alcoholic on the verge of taking his company down to the bottom of a whiskey bottle had no chance.

Romi's barely there grimace was quickly masked. "No."

"The waiting list for his services is a year out." Maxwell found himself offering the truth as an excuse, an unaccustomed effort to spare her feelings.

"No doubt you subverted it somehow."

Maxwell smiled. "Not a chance. The man's a martinet about his schedule and his client standards."

"Still, I'm surprised," Romi said, *her* intent to bait him obvious.

Something was definitely bothering her. "Are you?"

"You're a very opportunistic man." The edge to her voice was sharper than a chef's cleaver.

He couldn't deny it, didn't want to. His ability to identify and take advantage of opportunities was something that had helped Maxwell to build his business and his fortune to what they were today. A multimillionaire personally, his company, Black Information Technologies, or BIT, was valued at ten times his personal assets.

Not bad for a thirty-two-year-old bastard having no acknowledged ties to wealth, like Romi had been born with.

However, it was clear something about that character trait had upset Romi. Recently, if he wasn't mistaken. Since there was no way she could know about the plans he'd been considering for her father's company, it had to be something else.

Mentally going back through the events of the past week that others were aware of, Maxwell thought he might know. "You've spoken to Madison Archer."

"I talk to Maddie every day, several times a day." The increased annoyance in Romi's voice left no doubt he was on the right track.

Though he still was not sure *why* Romi would be upset with Maxwell for being offered the marriage-based business contract by Jeremy Archer.

"I can hardly be held accountable for her father's actions." Though he wouldn't hesitate to take advantage of the auspicious conditions Archer had provided, even if not for the opportunities the president of AIH had intended.

Romi crossed her arms, leaning back in a classic pose of annoyance. "Only your willingness to participate in them."

He took a moment to appreciate the way her stance pressed her small breasts together to create a shadow of tempting cleavage. Everything about her body turned him on. Thin, with modest curves, she was nevertheless one-hundred-percent enticing woman.

"I went to a meeting where Jeremy Archer offered a very

lucrative contract and your so-called sister-by-choice held her own very well." Though he wasn't prepared to tell Romi *how* Madison had kept her father in line.

Maxwell had plans for that information. Because he *was* an opportunistic bastard. Literally and figuratively.

Unless he'd misread Madison Archer, she had not shared her actions with her best friend.

Which created leverage for Maxwell with Romi. She would do anything to prevent her SBC from being harmed in any way. Even by Madison's own precipitous actions.

"You were willing to break your own rules for a price," Romi sneered.

Ah. Now he understood. Maxwell was actually a little surprised that Madison had shared his offer with Romi. The Archer heiress had never seriously considered it and he hadn't expected her to. That didn't mean he would deny himself the opportunity to give Viktor Beck a few seconds of doubt.

They'd been friends and competitors since early childhood.

Still, Romi was upset Maxwell had made the counteroffer. That might bode well for his own plans where she was concerned.

"And that price wasn't *love*." He laced the last word with his own brand of disgust.

The overly emotional and incredibly naive heiress thought that sentiment the only motivation worthy of note. Even after the loss of that *love* had nearly destroyed her own father and what remained of their family.

"More like thirty pieces of silver." Her blue gaze snapped with fire he wanted in his bed.

The small taste he'd had of her had only whetted an appetite Maxwell had come to accept would not be satisfied by anything but unfettered access to this woman alone.

"Your inference would imply I betrayed someone. I

didn't." He and Romi had gone their separate ways nearly a year ago.

"Your own integrity maybe."

"What is dishonest about a business deal where the terms are laid bare for everyone involved?"

"So, your 'no commitment' rule was only for me?" Romi's voice betrayed pained disappointment.

He didn't like hearing that from her. Even less than he'd liked the sound of "no thank you" spoken with a catch of desperation in her voice. "I didn't offer Madison the kind of commitment you believe you need."

"You offered to marry her."

"I offered a business arrangement without conjugal rights or the promise of fidelity."

"That's horrible." Romi was getting genuinely upset, her voice rising in agitation.

Soon, those around them would notice.

He took her by her elbow and began leading her toward the balcony doors. He was hoping the evening drop in temperature would mean it was deserted.

"Where are we going?" she asked, though she didn't try to pull away.

"Someplace more private than here."

Memory slashed across his brain...a similar question, an almost identical answer, but for a very different purpose.

He'd wanted to kiss her.

She'd been seething with an emotion very different from anger that time. She'd wanted the kiss, too.

Her response had nearly caused him to lose control of his own body for the first time since his initial foray into sex.

The balcony was as deserted as he'd hoped it would be, with only one other couple tucked away in the corner shadows at the opposite end. The low-level lighting and thirty feet separating the two couples insured a certain level of privacy so long as he and Romi did not raise their voices.

She shivered in the cool air and he moved them into the

corner, where strategically placed potted greenery acted as both a privacy screen and wind barrier.

Anyone looking closely would see them, but only from certain angles. The other couple was not at that angle.

Even without the wind, the evening air was still chilly.

He removed his jacket and tucked it around Romi like a cape. "Better?" he asked.

Nodding, Romi bit her lip in a gesture of vulnerability that nearly derailed his intention to *talk*.

"You didn't need to give me your coat." She pulled it closer, a clearly unconscious action in direct opposition to the words she spoke. "We won't be out here long. I'm not even sure why I came with you in the first place."

"Because you are angry I considered Jeremy Archer's business proposal and we need to talk about that."

"I don't know why."

He merely waited in silence.

Romi huffed out a sigh. "Maddie deserves better than a business marriage." She glared up at Maxwell with a mix of emotions he couldn't quite read. "You do, too."

"I do not find Madison particularly attractive. Foregoing conjugal rights would not have been a great sacrifice."

"She's beautiful."

"I find beauty in a different package." The red-headed Archer heiress was undeniably pleasing to the eye, but she did nothing for Maxwell personally.

He liked willowy figures, usually going for taller women because of his own six-foot-five-inch height. Though despite the foot difference in their height, Romi fit with him surprisingly well. He preferred dark hair and found her black tresses particularly appealing. Sharp elfin features were also unexpectedly attractive.

Before Romi, he'd never been drawn to blue eyes, but hers were so striking, so expressive, he found them intensely alluring. He liked knowing everything his sexual partners were feeling and thinking. Romi's eyes revealed what her charming verbal honesty did not.

And unlike her SBC, who rarely blushed at all, Romi's frequently pink cheeks—at least in his presence—that had nothing to do with her makeup were equally expressive.

"I just don't understand how you were willing to marry her." With a sound of frustration, Romi put her hand over her mouth, a sure sign she wished she hadn't said that out loud.

"I was willing to entertain the idea, but she wasn't interested in me as her future husband and I knew that before I ever made the offer of a marriage in name only."

"What? How did you know?"

"Madison Archer may be better at hiding her emotions than you, but there can be no doubt that only one man in that conference room had the remotest of chances in fulfilling the contract her father had drawn up."

Romi's smile was soft. "They're good together."

"Let's hope so." Viktor and Madison's engagement had already been announced, along with the whirlwind date set for their wedding.

He didn't know Madison Archer well, but what he knew of her, he respected and liked. And while many would look on Viktor as Maxwell's lifelong rival, the man who shared his Russian heritage was one of a select few Maxwell called friend.

Considering the fact that both people appeared to be entering the agreement with poorly hidden—to him at least—romantic aspirations and a long-term future together as their goal, Maxwell hoped it worked out for them.

He didn't believe in permanent romantic ties. He considered marriage like any other contract—to be kept in place for the duration of the benefit of both parties.

His mother had taught him from an early age to see romantic relationships as a means to an end. Natalya Black had always told her son that love was the biggest fairy tale of all.

She'd believed in Maxwell and told him he could do anything he set his mind to, but never give in to "so-called" love. It only weakened the afflicted and made them lose their focus.

Maxwell didn't know where his mother's life lessons had come from, but he knew his own and he'd discovered early on she was right.

Leaving Russia and her disapproving relatives for a new start in America had not included Natalya giving up her tendency to line her nest with the golden straw of cleverly chosen bed partners of defined duration.

The transience of the men in his mother's life had taught him one thing. There was no such thing as forever and anyone who believed in it was a fool.

They'd only come close one time. One man had made Natalya glow with something besides satisfaction in a well-chosen partner. The man had also taken a paternal interest in Maxwell as none of his mother's other affairs ever had or been allowed to.

For three years, Maxwell had a father figure show up at his activities, someone as interested in teaching him what it was to be a boy raised in America as his mother and those at the cultural center had been in exposing him to bits of his Russian heritage, someone besides a neighbor the school could call when Maxwell needed to go home early with the flu.

Then Carlyle's estranged wife had returned, along with his real son and daughter, and Maxwell never saw the man again. Natalya lost her glow, but not her determination to give Maxwell every chance life in America had to offer.

"Madison said she thought something about Perry's claims intrigued you." Romi frowned, her gaze searching.

Broken out of the unexpected reverie, Maxwell took a

moment to catch up. Then he said, "You know I like control in bed."

"I figured."

Yes, he hadn't hidden his preferences during their kisses and the touching. "I had no desire to take her to bed, therefore it follows my preference for control wasn't my reason for intrigue."

"Oh." Romi's frown turned to puzzlement. "Then why?"

"I found it interesting that Perry made the claims he did."

"The more salacious the story, the more money they would pay for it." The lovely heiress's tone dripped cynicism.

Maxwell's was a bit more derisive when he said, "Perry Timwater isn't capable of upholding a more dominant role in sex."

"How would you know?"

"I've met him." And what Maxwell had seen of the other man had neither impressed, nor inspired a desire to further their association. "He has neither the confidence, nor the attention to the needs of others to succeed in that role."

"I'm sure he's a selfish lover," Romi said with her customary direct honesty. "He was a very selfish friend."

"You are probably right." Maxwell felt his lips quirking as they often did in her presence.

Romi Grayson always entertained him, even when she didn't mean to. She intrigued him as much because of the attraction he felt for her as the fact she was so unlike him. He didn't understand her.

That was not something Maxwell was used to.

Understanding what motivated people was what made him so good in the business world. He knew how to identify a need and exploit it, without compromising his own sense of honor.

It might not be as shiny and uncomplicated as Viktor's, but Maxwell did have one.

Romi's mercurial nature made her an enigma. He'd been sure she would go for his offer of monogamy of limited duration, but she hadn't. Even more inexplicably, her reaction had told him the offer had hurt her in some way, which he hadn't expected and found he did not like.

"So, why *were* you intrigued?"

"Why do you think?" he prodded, wondering how much she'd really learned about him during their brief time of dating.

She paused and thought, which wasn't something anyone else would have expected from her. She came off as passionate and impetuous, but he'd learned that as much as she might appear to act without thought, Romi rarely ever did.

Finally, she said, "You've got more curiosity than any man I've ever met. The situation didn't make sense to you, something you aren't really on a first-name basis with. So you wanted to understand it."

He nodded, not really surprised she guessed his reaction so easily. He'd learned that she studied him with as much attention as he had any business rival in his career.

"The stories themselves were a puzzle," Maxwell agreed. "Despite both you and Madison Archer's penchant for making it into the media spotlight, neither of you are known for sexual exploits."

Something he should have paid closer attention to before making his offer to her. He should have realized that the reason her sex life was never speculated on in the media was because she didn't have one.

That innocence wasn't going to leave her open to the kind of liaison Maxwell was used to negotiating with his lovers.

Which meant that if he wanted Romi, and the year apart had shown him that at present no one else would suffice, he would have to figure out a different arrangement.

One they could both live with.

If his plans included a measure of what he thought might well be irresistible persuasion, well, his honor didn't require a level playing field.

Winning was key. Full stop.

CHAPTER TWO

"AND YOU FOUND *that* intriguing?" Romi demanded.

Max was amused by the fact she and Madison weren't known for their sexual promiscuity, no doubt following that particular line of reasoning to its correct conclusion. They weren't known for it because they'd never been sexually promiscuous.

The most experience Romi had in that regard had been with Max himself.

"Not so much, no." Max actually managed to look more or less abashed. "It brought to light some home truths. That's all."

"What do you mean?" Like she didn't know.

He *had* worked it out. If there had been anything to write about her or Madison's sex life, media vultures would have done it. Therefore there was *nothing* to write about.

Max's gorgeous features twisted with a cynical smile. "Do you really want me to spell it out for you?"

"Maybe not." Romi stifled a sigh, the certainty that she spent a little too much of her life avoiding those home truths he was talking about pricking at her until it drew blood.

She wanted to talk about the reason her nonexistent lovers were never discussed in the media even less than she wanted to discuss her father's deteriorating condition. Even with Maddie. If Romi pretended everything was okay, maybe it would be.

The fact that she spent a great deal of her waking hours

trying to right injustices and excesses of the world she lived in, but could not face her own family's brokenness, did not escape her.

"What is the matter?" Max asked in a tone she would have called genuine concern from anyone else.

From him? It probably indicated that moment his inner shark smelled blood in the water.

"Nothing."

"That is not true."

"Does it matter?" she asked with a heavy dose of skepticism.

He adjusted her closer. "Yes."

They were just standing there. No enemies, or even pernicious media in sight. And yet, his big, handsome body felt like a shield between her and the rest of the world. That was one of the most dangerous things about Maxwell Black: how safe she felt in his presence.

He was a full-on predator, but he made her feel protected.

Talk about a rich and active fantasy life.

"Why?" Why would her feelings make any difference to him?

How could they? She wasn't anything to him. Not anything at all.

His pewter gaze trapped hers. "You matter to me."

"No. I don't believe you." As a potential bed partner she might have had some value, but they hadn't been anything like friends.

"You will."

"What? Wait…" He was talking like they had a future.

"You look confused, my sweet little activist."

"I'm not *your* anything." And if she needed reminding as much, or more, than he did, well…she wasn't admitting anything out loud.

"Aren't you?"

"No."

"So, you've been dating."

She opened her mouth to say of course she had, but couldn't force word one of the untruth past her lips. Romi might be a professional at avoidance, but tongue-tied only began to describe what happened to her when she tried to tell a bald-faced lie.

Especially to people she cared about. Prevaricate? Yes. Obfuscate? Definitely. Sidestep? She had the full bag of tricks. Out-and-out lie? Not a chance.

"My dating life is none of your business."

"You don't have one."

"So you say." Right. Turn it back on him without confirming or denying. She would have a made a good spy.

Except for that whole "inability to lie" thing.

"I do say. Name one man you have dated since you turned down my offer."

She glared up at Max, wanting so much just to pull a name out of the air. Any name. But she could not do it.

It just wasn't in her. Her dad said she got that trait from her mother. Romi wished she could remember Jenna Grayson, but she'd only been three when her mom died.

"I bet you could name a hundred." Redirection was her friend.

"Not even a half dozen."

He was still a handful ahead of her. "You work too many hours."

It was a problem.

"You think so?"

"I know so." She'd seen the evidence in the short time they'd been dating.

He didn't move, but suddenly he felt closer, like he was taking up more of the space between them than he had been. "Running a company like BIT cannot be done in a forty-hour work week."

"It could if you weren't so intent on being king of the world." She found herself wanting to lean into him and just let him hold her.

How crazy was that?

Max's laughter washed through her, warming in a way even his tuxedo jacket did not. "I promise, I am not trying to be king of the world."

"Just your part of it."

"Well, I have competition."

"So you say." She wasn't sure she believed it.

Maxwell had a ruthless streak that meant he would always be top dog, even if it meant a dirty, bloody battle to get there.

"None of the women I have dated in the past year rated a callback audition."

"Poor them."

Max's smile was predatory and just a little bit devastating. "You think so."

She knew so. Walking away from him had been one of the most difficult things Romi had ever done, but no way was she giving him a chance to own her heart only to break it.

As he was guaranteed to do.

"I enjoyed dating you." A huge understatement, it still came out easily because it was also the truth.

"As I enjoyed our time together."

"Good?" Embarrassed the word had come out more a question than statement, Romi felt a blush crawl up her neck.

"Not good. You turned me down."

"We wanted different things." And apparently she hadn't thought to offer him part of a company to get what she wanted.

Visions of doing just that caused a bubble of hysterical laughter to nearly burst out.

It was all she could do to hold the humor in.

She couldn't hold back a few mocking words however. "Too bad my dad wasn't selling my hand in marriage, huh?"

Max tugged her close, his head tipping down. "I was thinking that exact thing."

"You jerk." She was laughing as she said the words, not meaning them, just responding in kind to his sarcasm.

But it meant her lips were parted when his mouth landed against hers.

Heat suffused her as her traitorous body melted into his without forethought or even permission from the thinking part of her brain. Forced suddenly into blatant recognition of a year's long starvation of her senses, she returned his kiss with a hunger she'd done her best to pretend did not exist.

Voracious now, she had no hope of holding back the tide of feeling crashing over her.

It was the cost of ignoring emotions rather than facing them.

She wanted this man with every fiber of her being, no matter how much her brain told her it was a bad idea.

A spectacularly, out-of-this-world, *really* bad idea.

Her lips did not agree as they moved against his, her tongue eager as it met his, her body pliant to his touch.

She skimmed her hands up his hard chest, mapping the shape of muscles honed by workouts that would make a tri-athlete pause. Singeing her fingertips with electric warmth, the heat of his body translated through the smooth fabric of his dress shirt.

She brushed over tiny, hardened nubs and she reveled in the proof of her effect on him.

With a feral groan, Max flexed his lower body toward hers and she had even more potent proof in the press of his clearly excited, intimidatingly large shaft against her. It couldn't be comfortable for him to be trapped in his clothes in that condition, but he didn't complain or pull away.

Unheeded, his expensive, handmade tuxedo jacket fell from her shoulders as she wrapped her hands around his neck and pressed into him, chest to thigh. Was it possible to feel sparks in every single nerve ending of where her body met his?

She didn't know if it was some kind of domino effect, but that's what it felt like to her.

As her body exploded with delight in that simple but very intimate touch, the kiss went nuclear.

Their mouths ate at each other, his hands moved over her back, down along her sides, over her bottom…everywhere. Hers locked behind his head as she undulated against him—giving friction, receiving the stimulation she needed. It was insane. The way she responded to his nearness, the unending and increasing desire for more and more and more.

Sensations she'd dreamt about almost nightly and pretended to forget in the morning, but hadn't experienced in a year, roared through her in a conflagration as unstoppable as the brush fires that raged in the south every summer.

It burned the walls of her defenses to cinders. All she could do was hold on and hope not to be consumed completely.

It was Max that broke the kiss, Max that took a step back, Max that held her away from him when she would have followed.

Feeling too much desire to be embarrassed, Romi demanded, "Why?"

He wanted her. She'd felt it. If she looked down, she'd see it, even in the dim shadows of the balcony.

"The next time we have sex, it will be in a bed and I won't stop until you've climaxed with me inside you." His breath panted in irregular intervals, but his deep voice was infused with absolute certainty.

She barely bit back the *when* that wanted to pop out of her mouth.

Oh, wow. Yeah. Not a good idea.

But she wanted it. So bad. She shook with the need to continue what they started, for just the experience of being held in his arms again.

"That can't happen." She wished her voice had even a modicum of certainty in it.

Some little bit of the self-preservation that lay in ashes around her.

"That's a lie and you don't do those."

She opened her mouth to deny his words, but darned if he wasn't right. "Please, don't do this to me, Max."

"What don't you want me to do, Romi, my sweet virgin?" Why did those words sound so hot in his voice? "Turn you on? You weren't complaining a second ago."

She couldn't deny it. Wasn't sure she wanted to, even if she could. "Neither were you."

But he'd stopped and she hadn't even thought to try. Darn him.

"No, and I never will."

Why did he have to say things like that? Things that could make her hope when hope and this man did *not* go together. "We still want different things."

"Are you so sure? If I hadn't stopped, you would have let me take you here and now."

He was talking about sex when she was referring to a relationship. And he knew it. "Do you get some sick thrill out of rubbing in my own weakness to me?"

"It's not a weakness, *milaya.*"

"So you say." Her words lacked conviction, but he knew what using his Russian endearments on her did to Romi.

It wasn't just the fact he called her lovely, but his possessive claim on her and how he only used this word on her. She'd asked him, annoyed when she thought he was just calling her the same thing he did every other woman he slept with.

He'd admitted he never used the Russian endearments with other women.

She hadn't asked why because he had seemed less than thrilled about the realization and she hadn't wanted him to stop.

Now she wished she had.

"So I know," he responded, no lack of conviction in *his* tone. "Your passion is amazing."

"You stopped." It couldn't have been that amazing.

"Because I want something better for your first time."

"You're making some big assumptions there."

"Are you going to try to deny your innocence?"

"No." And they were back to this again because this man never let Romi run her repertoire of avoidance techniques about the important stuff. "My first time isn't going to be with a man who puts a sell-by date on his girlfriends before the relationship even starts."

"And yet your first time *will* be with me."

"I was talking about you," she informed him sarcastically.

"No. You were talking about a circumstance, not a man."

She stepped away from him and hated how cold that made her feel, and not just because of the goose bumps on her arms. "Are you trying to confuse me on purpose?"

"No, *milaya*. Not at all. I'm just telling the truth."

"And what truth is that?" She was going to regret asking, she just knew it.

"That you will be in my bed very soon."

"Without a sell-by date?" she asked with a tiny kernel of hope that felt almost like a betrayal.

But could he really have spent the last year wanting her like she'd been wanting him, enough to break his own set-in-cement rules?

"Not as a boyfriend."

"What does *that* mean?" Was he trying to say he didn't want any commitment at all?

A one-night stand? For the loss of her virginity? And why was that even a little bit tempting?

He never answered her question, just picked up his suit jacket and shook it out before putting it back on. Quality cut and fabric showed almost no effect from its sojourn on the balcony floor.

Somehow she found herself back inside dancing with the man, ignoring the glares of envy sent her way and doing her best to do the same to her own body's weakness in the face of Max's nearness.

He set out to entertain and charm, succeeding to the point that she let him drive her home instead of calling for her father's car and driver.

He pulled the Maserati, a different one than he'd been driving the year before, to a purring halt in front of her dad's mansion. This one had a backseat.

"Still living with your father?" he asked, though he had to know, or why else would they be here?

"Yes."

Max nodded. "No desire to live on your own?"

"He needs me." It was an admission, but not one that would surprise an American tycoon with surprisingly deep Russian roots.

Romi didn't even share with Maddie how bad things had gotten for her dad, but a year ago? She'd told Maxwell Black.

On their second date. Maybe that was why he'd put the sell-by date on their relationship after their third one.

But no, that was just the way Max ran his love life, or sex life really. The man didn't believe in love. Well, that wasn't quite accurate.

He believed the emotion was real enough, just refused to ever let himself feel it.

Romi wished *she* had the ability to turn her heart off.

But it was never going to happen.

"You are a good daughter." His pewter eyes warmed with sincerity.

It was almost surreal. "What, no admonishment to leave him to work it out on his own?"

"What have I ever said that implied I did not take the obligations of family seriously?" Max actually sounded a little offended.

Feeling convicted for letting her own insecurities spill over onto him, Romi said, "Nothing."

She knew he cared deeply for his mother.

Max had never been hesitant to admit he supported Natalya Black financially. They might live separately, but Romi had no doubt that if his mother needed to live with him, they would be sharing a residence right now. No questions, no lesser options.

"We share a dedication to family."

"What we have of them," she agreed.

Romi didn't know why, but Max and his mother had no connection to their family back in Russia. He'd never mentioned his father, much less the man's family, so Romi had always assumed they were either all gone or like her father's family.

Estranged.

"I still see my mom's family yearly." Unlike the Graysons, who had turned their back on Harry when he'd married a woman from a decidedly middle-class background instead of old money, the Lawtons had remained in their daughter's life and that of her husband and child.

Albeit on a more limited basis than Romi had always wanted.

"Why only once a year?" Max asked, like he was reading her mind.

She shrugged, looking away from him. "They only came to visit when my mom was alive. Since then, I've gone to stay with my grandparents for a couple of weeks every summer."

But she and her father had never been invited to share the major holidays with them. Romi didn't know if that was because he'd made it clear in some way he wasn't interested, or if they weren't, and she'd never really tried to find out.

It was enough she got a taste of the family that had made her mom the person she'd been. Even if that person was someone Romi would never know.

She'd enjoyed the different kind of living, sharing a room with the sewing machine and her grandmother's craft projects, sleeping on the floor in the family room with her cousins when they stayed over. No servants, no cars and drivers, no shopping in exclusive boutiques.

Lots of summer barbecues, playing in a yard maintained better by her grandfather than any gardener her dad had ever employed.

"Why don't any of them come to visit you?" Max asked.

She didn't really know, but had made her own internal excuses. "It's a long trip."

"A few hours by plane."

"Still."

"It's a different world for them, isn't it?"

She nodded. She'd finally come to realize as an adult that her mom's family found her life as an heiress—her bedroom that was a three-room suite in a multimillion-dollar mansion, all of the trappings of wealth—too foreign for comfort.

She thought maybe they hadn't been any happier that Jenna had married Harry than the Graysons. The Lawtons just hadn't turned their backs on their daughter.

Her grandparents were political activists like Romi, but unlike her, they had little affection or respect for the people that had populated Romi's life since birth.

Old money wealth, *big business*, they were dirty words to her grandparents.

Romi had always wanted to make a difference, but she'd never felt the need to destroy the system to rebuild it.

Her grandparents had spent a month living in a tent during Occupy Wall Street. Her aunts and uncles weren't as antiwealth and antiestablishment, but made no bones about the fact they preferred their suburban lives over Romi's in San Francisco.

"Your cousins could come to visit, couldn't they?" Max asked, like it mattered to him.

She didn't know why it should. Romi shrugged. "I'm not as close with them as I was when I was little."

Not like they were to each other.

Her mother had been the youngest and all of her cousins were at least five years older than Romi. Most were married with children, all were established in careers and lives that did not lend themselves to visiting a single cousin cross country that they barely knew.

Max made a sound that in anyone else would have been a sigh. He made it seem more like a nonverbal admission. "My family turned their back on my mother because she chose to break with tradition."

"She married an American?"

"No."

"But Black…"

"Is not a Russian name. She changed it from Blokov when she immigrated with me. She wanted no reminder of the family who found it so easy to reject her because she lived her life differently than they wanted her to."

"I'm sorry. She's a pretty neat lady."

Romi had met Natalya Black at more than one charity function she'd attended with her son. Romi had found the older Russian woman still quite beautiful and very charming.

"She is pragmatic."

"She raised you. I imagine she is." Romi had never known anyone as compartmentalized and rationally logical as Max.

Max quirked his brow. "Is that a compliment or a complaint?"

"Neither, really." Romi grinned cheekily. "It just is."

"Now, you sound like a proper Russian pragmatist."

"What about your dad?" Romi asked, surprised at herself.

But she'd regretted all the questions she hadn't asked a year ago too much to make the same mistake again.

"My mother has never named him, though I have often thought his name must be something similar to mine, as Maxwell is hardly Russian."

"Maybe she just wanted to break away from her homeland and embrace her new life in America."

"We emigrated when I was a year old."

"Oh."

He smiled, no indication the discussion hurt him. "Some things just are, right?"

"Right." But somehow she was sure this man would never allow a child of his to grow up not even knowing his name.

They said good-night, with Max's assertion he would see her again soon sounding more like a threat than a promise.

CHAPTER THREE

MAXWELL DRANK A glass of very good champagne and watched Romi Grayson fulfill her role as maid of honor for Madison Beck, née Archer, with her usual flair.

Adorned with a tiara every bit as ornate, if significantly smaller than Madison's, Romi's smooth bob of hair glistened in a fall of black silk around her face. Large but tasteful diamonds in a classic setting twinkled in her earlobes. She wore no other jewelry with the designer silk gown of blue that exactly matched her pretty eyes and was cut to complement Madison's 1950s vintage gown.

Romi flicked a look at him and he made no effort to hide the fact he watched her. Pleasure zinged through him at the blush that tinted her cheeks.

She looked away, but her azure gaze returned to meet his almost immediately.

He let one eyelid slide closed in a slow wink, allowing his lips to almost tilt into a smile.

The blush darkened and he could see the breath she took. Imagining he could hear the soft gasp of air that followed, he started across the room toward her.

A hand landed on his arm and he barely broke stride to shake his head decisively at a woman he'd flirted with previously on a couple of occasions. The sister of a man who owned one of the major companies in Silicon Valley, she was a contact worth cultivating.

But not right now.

Romi had not moved so much as an inch since he'd started toward her, waiting as if she stood inside a bubble of her own.

No one approached her when she'd spent the last hours talking to *everyone*. But there was something ethereal about her in that moment and Maxwell knew he wasn't the only one who felt it.

He stopped in front of her, his hand out. "Dance with me."

This time he heard the small catch of air. "I…"

"You know you want to."

"We don't always want what is best for us."

He shook his head, not buying it. "No word games right now, Romi. Just dance with me."

"You are demanding."

He shrugged and pulled her into his arms, not surprised when she didn't object and not even a little shocked when her body unhesitatingly molded to his. They reacted to each other in a physical way that was almost mystical.

If he believed in that sort of thing.

The music was slow and he pulled her body close into the shelter of his own so they could move together in a special kind of intimacy.

"Did you enjoy the wedding?" she asked in the soft tone that haunted his dreams.

"How did you know I was in attendance?" The invitation to the reception had not surprised Maxwell, but the invite to the wedding had.

He knew it was Viktor's doing. Or perhaps the older Becks. They considered Maxwell *family* by dint of their shared heritage and years spent as friendly neighbors.

"I seem to have some kind of homing device where you are concerned," Romi admitted in a voice that didn't sound either particularly happy or bothered by that reality. "I'm pretty sure Maddie didn't know you were there."

"It was predominately family." The other heiress wouldn't have been looking for his face among her other guests.

"Yes." It was a statement, but with a question underlying the agreement.

"I grew up with Viktor."

"I didn't know that." Romi looked up, her blue eyes searching his face. "It should be hard to imagine you as a child, but it isn't."

"I do not know why. Everyone is a child at some point."

"Are you sure?" she teased.

He frowned, but he wasn't actually even a little annoyed. "I spent time in diapers and playing in sandboxes just like anyone else. I promise."

"No popping fully formed into existence as a corporate tycoon?" she taunted.

"You are feeling feisty, aren't you?"

She shrugged. "I just like teasing you."

"I noticed." No one else but his mother ever had.

And Natalya Black was too practical to be playful all that often, even with her only child.

"I was a child like everyone else," he assured her. "You said yourself you could picture it."

Her smile was nothing short of wicked. "A child surely, but not like everyone else. Not you."

"I was. I even wanted to be a fireman when I was a little boy." A common aspiration among his classmates.

Romi grinned. "I wanted to be a princess."

He was charmed. "Right now, you look like you got your wish."

She laughed, the sound joyous and instantly addictive. He couldn't help but join her.

"Did you really say something so naff?"

"What is naff about it?" But he knew. In any other instance, he'd think another man telling a woman she looked like a princess was completely cheesy.

The truth made it something else.

"You said I look like a princess," she pointed out with patent disbelief and a lot of leftover humor.

"I did."

Her eyes widened innocently, and she asked, "Aren't you even a little embarrassed?"

"Corporate kings don't get embarrassed, didn't you know that? Especially when we speak the truth."

She gasped and went silent for several seconds before asking, "When did you realize you'd rather be king than a firefighter?"

Oh, she did like avoiding things that made her uncomfortable. He only let her get away with it sometimes. This would be one of them.

It should be an easy question to answer, but Maxwell realized he wasn't sure when he'd given up his aspirations of saving lives and instead decided he wanted a different kind of power. "Somewhere between wanting to be a super hero and realizing Batman had to be as rich as the royal family to do the things he did."

"Did you ever stop wanting to be a superhero?"

"Corporate kings don't save the world."

"Don't they?" She was very serious all of a sudden. "Black Information Technologies is one of the most sustainable of the Fortune 500 companies."

"It's a matter of practicality."

"Why did I know you'd say something like that?"

"Because I grew out of my desire to be Batman."

"Good. His backstory is too dark anyway."

He laughed, once again delighted by her outlook.

Romi grew serious. "I can't imagine a company like BIT springing up out of a half-baked idea and a lot of ingenuity."

"No. I planned the start of the company and its trajectory very carefully from the very beginning." He'd begun the plans the day he learned of the final concession his mother had negotiated from his father.

A multimillion-dollar settlement for Maxwell on his eighteenth birthday.

Maxwell wasn't supposed to know who his father was. Growing up, all he'd been able to guess was the man had been rich and powerful enough to facilitate his former mistress's immigration to America.

Maxwell had assumed his father had been American as well, though his mother's plans to move to this country could well have had nothing to do with the homeland of her son's father. Maxwell had learned he was right when he'd hired Sebastian Hawk's international security and detective agency to find out who the man was.

Hawk's agency was *the* organization to go to for security and information. Maxwell had gone to them when he'd first opened his company and had met the owner a year later. Sebastian Hawk was a self-made millionaire who still took an interest in how his company was run.

Maxwell had more than doubled his initial capital and wanted to return the settlement to the father who had never had an interest in meeting, much less recognizing, his son.

Maxwell had discovered his father was a high-ranking diplomat from a very powerful and obscenely wealthy American family with public servant ties back to the revolutionary era. Married, with children older than his illegitimate son, the man had had a great deal to lose if Maxwell's existence came to light.

Pointedly changing the direction of his own thoughts, Maxwell said, "I stopped wanting to be a fireman after visiting the fire station on a school field trip."

"That's funny." Romi tilted her head to the side and observed him with interest even as her body moved against his to the rhythm of the music. "That's when kids usually decide they want to be one."

"Most of the other children in my class did. I've never wanted to be part of a crowd."

"So you decided you couldn't be a fireman because everyone else wanted to be one?" she asked, humor lacing her lovely voice.

"Exactly."

She grinned. "You wanted to be special."

"Are you saying I am not?"

"Oh, no, Your Majesty," she said facetiously. "You are definitely in a class all by yourself."

"Not alone maybe, but not like *everyone* else."

"Firefighters are actually a very small percentage of our population." She pointed out that fact like maybe he didn't know.

"Yes, they are a rarified breed as well, and definitely to be admired and respected. However, I like control far too much to have a job dealing with either nature's vagaries or that of human error, which I have no power to prevent."

"There is that." Romi shook her head. "Have you always been such a control freak?"

"My mother would say yes."

Romi didn't appear bothered by that admission. "I kind of like you this way."

He wondered if she would say that after he laid out his latest plan for her.

"I am glad," he said.

"Although I think the more appropriate term would be *Corporate Tsar* rather than *King*."

"You think so? Because I was born in Russia?"

"Because you have the heart of a tsar, I think."

He could not deny it.

He kept her in his arms by the simple expedient of continuing to dance for another thirty minutes. Even during the faster music and she never complained.

A couple of men tried to cut in, but Maxwell refused to offer the polite retreat and simply danced her away. When a woman tried the same, wanting to dance with him, he turned her down as well.

"You really aren't controlled by social niceties, are you?" Romi asked after the last one.

"You knew this about me."

She nodded with something like satisfaction. "I'll admit, I don't mind in this instance."

"I'm glad to hear that, but admit to being curious as to why." Just something about the way she'd spoken, he thought there was a story behind her words.

"Have you ever danced with JD?" she asked, referring to the last man Maxwell had simply ignored in his attempt to partner Romi.

Maxwell gave a short bark of laughter. "No."

"He's grabby. Though I suppose if he danced with you he wouldn't be." Her giggle was very smug.

"You think you are funny, don't you?"

"Why yes, I do."

Maxwell's eyes narrowed. "You're saying he tried to touch you?"

"Nothing serious. He just pretends he doesn't realize my waist is several inches above the curve of my behind."

"I'll break his hand." Maxwell was shocked by the words.

Not the sentiment. He knew he was unacceptably protective of this woman, but to express it out loud wasn't something he usually did.

"Not necessary." She snuggled in. "I can be a very klutzy dancer when I need to be."

The effort it took to hold back further imprecations did not make him happy.

Romi allowed herself to relax in Maxwell's arms while they danced longer than she probably should have. But it felt so good, so *safe*.

Eventually, she had to look up and scan the room for her dad.

He was talking to Jeremy Archer, his movements animated, on the verge of exaggerated, and his expression belligerent.

Not good.

Stifling her regret at the action, Romi pushed herself away from Max. "I need to go check on my father."

The self-made tycoon didn't argue, for which she was grateful.

She wasn't sure how she felt a second later, though, when he said, "I'll come with you."

"That's not necessary," she said by rote rather than from feeling.

He didn't bother to reply, just took her arm and started toward Jeremy and Romi's dad.

Harry Grayson's voice was elevated, his speech slightly slurred. "I don't need your advice, Jeremy. One of us actually grieved the passing of his wife. It's affected my business, but I'm far from bankrupt."

This was not good. Anytime her dad started talking about Romi's deceased mother, things had a way of sliding downhill fast.

Preparing to intervene, Romi was nonplussed when Max's deep voice dropped into the tense silence. "Good evening, gentlemen. May I offer my congratulations, Jeremy? Madison makes a beautiful bride and Viktor Beck is a very good man."

His eyes widened in surprise, but the business mogul nodded his gray head in acknowledgement. "Thank you, Black."

Romi ignored Jeremy Archer in favor of her own father, and not just because it was clear the time had come to go. But she hadn't forgiven Jeremy for the way he treated Madison when the whole Perry debacle happened.

Romi had never thought the man was much of a father before that, but her opinion of him had dropped even lower.

"Dad," she said to Harry Grayson, "I'm getting tired. I'd like to go, if that's all right."

Her father turned a confused gaze on her. "You were having fun dancing."

"But I wore her out," Max smoothly inserted, with one of those conspiratorial smiles men seemed so adept at giving each other.

Particularly the men she knew.

Her dad gave Jeremy an angry look and then nodded at Romi. "Okay, kitten. I'll call for the car."

"No need. I'm happy to drop you both off."

"In your Maserati?" While he no longer drove the two-door, purely sporty model, and this one had a backseat, Max had been drinking champagne before they started dancing.

"I've got a car and driver and I've already texted him. He'll be waiting for us when we get outside."

"You're very efficient." And Romi wasn't sure she meant that as a compliment.

The wry twist to Max's lips said he guessed that. "Oh, I am."

"A little too coldly efficient, if you ask me," Jeremy Archer had the audacity to say.

"Says the man with antifreeze instead of blood pumping through his veins," her dad said with surprising clarity, both of thought and speech.

Jeremy's face contorted with annoyance. "You need to go home and let your daughter pour you into bed, Gray."

"What I need—" her father started to say.

"We'll chalk this conversation up to the tactlessness that can come from longstanding friendship," Max said in a tone that warned his patience was not limitless. "Agreed?"

In a move that shocked Romi, both her dad and Jeremy nodded. Grudgingly, but they agreed all the same.

"Good." Max gave Jeremy a look that Romi couldn't quite interpret. "From now on, you don't need to worry about the viability of Grayson Enterprises. It is not up for grabs, nor will it be facing bankruptcy anytime in the near or distant future."

Wow. That was quiet a promise. And an odd one for Max to make.

Her dad hadn't said anything about BIT and Grayson going into business together, but his expression didn't look nearly as confused as Romi felt.

In fact, the expression he'd turned toward his oldest friend and sometimes rival was nothing short of triumphant. "That's right, and Romi's not *my* investment capital in this deal, either."

What deal? What had her father and Max been talking about?

Jeremy looked first startled and then concerned. "You're merging?"

But her dad didn't answer, finally showing some sense of discretion. He even congratulated Jeremy on his daughter's marriage. "They're a good, solid couple, no matter how they got together."

Romi believed that, too. It was the only reason she'd accepted Maddie's request to be her maid of honor. Her SBC deserved the best and a chance at true happiness.

Romi believed Viktor Beck was that for Maddie.

Maddie didn't try to convince her to stay longer when Romi told her they were leaving. She didn't even voice concern at the fact Romi and her father were doing so in the company of Maxwell Black.

Maddie just hugged her hard and thanked Romi for being the best sister a woman could ever choose *or* be born with.

When they arrived at her home, Max walked to the door with Romi and her father.

He stopped outside. "I'm not going to come in tonight, but I'll be by tomorrow morning to talk."

Romi wasn't sure if he was talking to her or her dad, but Harry nodded so she figured it was him.

"I'll look forward to it," her dad said before stepping inside.

Max nodded, his masculine lips set in a firm line. Then

he turned to Romi. "I would like to take you to lunch afterward."

"Oh, I—"

"The time for running is done, Ramona. We have things we need to discuss."

She didn't bother telling him she didn't like being addressed by her full name. That minor annoyance was nothing compared to the threat of *talking*. "We did all our discussing a year ago."

"Circumstances change."

She wrapped her arms around herself, trying to hold the heat in. "I'm pretty sure ours haven't."

"And yet I am requesting your company all the same." He reached out and tucked her wrap more tightly around her.

"Sounds more like a demand to me."

He shrugged. "I have been accused."

"Yeah. That's believable."

"Then believe me when I tell you that we have things, important things, we need to discuss." He brushed the back of his fingers down her cheek.

Romi shivered, but not from the cold this time. "What are they?"

"I'm sure you can guess."

"Max…" But she didn't know what she wanted to say, where she wanted *this* conversation to go.

She'd spent a year doing her best to forget Maxwell Black and it hadn't worked.

The silence stretched between them before he leaned down and kissed her firmly, but quickly. "Tomorrow, Romi. Block out your afternoon."

"For lunch?" she asked breathlessly and unable to do a thing about that fact.

"For me."

"I'm not making any promises, Max."

"I am, Romi. Both to myself and to you. You will be mine."

The words should have made her nervous. Should have scared her right of her wits really, but Romi liked them too much. Her secret fantasies all revolved around this man.

She touched her lips, still tingling from the kiss. "Tomorrow."

Without another word, Max turned and went down the steps with a purposeful stride.

Romi moved restlessly in her bed. She'd left her father sleeping on the sofa in his study, the usual wool throw covering him.

She should be thinking about her best friend and the irrevocable step Maddie had taken in marrying Viktor Beck. Or if not that, Romi should be worrying about the problems with her dad's company that Jeremy Archer clearly felt worth accosting her father over at his own daughter's wedding reception.

But all of that bubbled in its own cauldron of stress at the periphery of the thoughts consuming her.

Maxwell Black said she was going to be his.

He knew she wanted a commitment. The hope of a future, not a guarantee, but at least the possibility. Okay *probability*. But she wasn't looking for promises as much as the likelihood of them being made down the road.

None of which had he been willing to offer a year ago.

No, he'd presented the possibility of six months to a year of sexual pleasure and intermittent companionship, with the clear and nonnegotiable understanding that they would go their separate ways after a year.

She'd turned him down flat.

And it had not been easy, though she'd tried very hard not to let Max see just how difficult she'd found it to utter that single-syllable word. *No*.

But her heart had been on the line and she was smart enough to know it.

She hadn't suddenly gone stupid, so why had she agreed to meet with Max?

Romi didn't have a reason, at least not a good one.

She still wanted him. She still found him the most intriguing and attractive man she'd ever met.

Maxwell Black was her Kryptonite and that scared the willies out of her.

Some people, after growing up the way she had, watching her dad pine for her dead mother and slowly come apart, would have been determined never to go through that themselves.

Romi had taken the opposite view. She wanted that kind of devotion directed at her. She knew what it was to be loved.

Her dad was flawed. Some might even say weak, but he loved Romi with the best that was in him.

His drinking had taken its toll, but it hadn't all been bad. Harry Grayson had given his daughter the finest he had to give and she was grateful.

His company might have suffered, but she'd never once doubted her dad's love.

She was determined that the man she married one day would love her with that same kind of devotion. Hopefully *without* a past grief to overcome and an addiction to alcohol.

Max's intensity and dedication to her pleasure had tricked her into thinking once that he might just be that guy.

He'd disabused her of that belief. With prejudice. No matter how he saw it.

So, why was she meeting him tomorrow?

Because she couldn't help herself.

For the daughter of an alcoholic that was not just a little worrisome.

That was terrifying.

She had to wrest back control of her life.

Because she *wasn't* her dad.

Romi was her own person, with her own strengths and

her own weaknesses. She wasn't going to let Max be one of them.

Even if she craved him with a desire embedded to the very marrow of her bones.

Maybe what she needed was her own deal.

Her own offer with a set of parameters that weren't going to leave her heart bleeding out when he walked away.

CHAPTER FOUR

MAXWELL WALKED INTO Harry Grayson's study, with the certain knowledge that he was looking forward to his lunch meeting with Romi much more.

However, this one was necessary if he wanted the next one to end the way he planned for it to.

Dressed casually in a sweater over his dress shirt and tie, his trousers creased perfectly, Harry Grayson's slightly reddened eyes were the only indicator of his excesses the night before. "Good morning, Maxwell. Have a seat. I'll ring for coffee."

"Thank you." In other circumstances, Maxwell might have refused the offer of hospitality, but he was sure the older man could do with a shot of caffeine.

Maxwell was actually a little relieved that things hadn't progressed to the point where Grayson had offered him a drink at nine in the morning. He waited quietly while Grayson called his housekeeper and ordered a tray of the hot beverage.

Grayson's hand trembled only slightly as he hung up the phone. "I looked over the contract you sent over."

"Good." That was another positive sign.

"It's a favorable contract."

"To both parties." Maxwell didn't do charity when it came to business.

"Why?"

"What?"

"Why Grayson Enterprises? Surely there are better companies for this sort of merger. Black Information Technologies isn't just solvent. You're growing with ROIs other companies would kill for in this climate."

"Yes." Maxwell didn't deny it.

There was no point. He'd worked hard, and smart, to make his company what it was today.

"So, you have nearly unlimited options for this kind of merger. I'm not so blind I don't realize my company probably isn't the best of them."

"I plan to marry your daughter."

The stark words hit the older man like a blow. He sat back in his chair like Maxwell's strike had been physical rather than verbal. "I'm not Jeremy Archer. I'm not selling my daughter to insure the future of my company."

"And I am not trying to buy her." Not that Maxwell considered Viktor's marriage to Madison in that light.

The man wanted control of AIH, but he wanted the woman, too.

"Do you love her?" Grayson demanded.

"That is between Romi and myself."

"She's my daughter. I want her to be happy."

"Do you?"

"Of course I do. How can you ask that? I'm no Jeremy Archer," he said again, like that particular point was one that needed making. Maybe it was. To him. "I'm not selling Romi to save a company that isn't on the brink of bankruptcy, no matter what that bastard likes to imply."

Maxwell didn't bother reminding Grayson he'd already said as much. No matter how together he *looked*, going to bed drunk night after night took its toll on the man's thought processes.

"But you are vulnerable to takeover." The fact Maxwell didn't have to be here making a merger offer could be left unspoken.

Grayson wasn't stupid, even if he wasn't thinking with the same sharp reasoning he'd once been known for.

Just nearly constantly inebriated.

"Romi isn't part of this deal."

Did he think if he kept saying it that would make it truer? "No, she isn't, but your sobriety is."

"What? That wasn't in the contract." Grayson looked down at the contract Maxwell's office had sent over two days before like it might jump up and attack.

Maxwell pulled a sheaf of papers from his briefcase. "No, it's in the codicil I've got here."

Last night he'd realized that Romi might well need more than the impetus he'd arranged for her acquiescence to his plans. If he wanted to give Romi something more than just saving her father's company from the other predators, he would keep that particular motivation to himself.

Grayson paled sickly as he read the codicil. "I don't have to agree to this. My life is my business."

"And yet I've decided to make it *my* business."

"Like my company."

"Would you rather be having this discussion with Jeremy Archer?"

"More like Viktor Beck."

"Viktor wouldn't consider the merger. He'd go for the takeover." Because in his own way, Viktor Beck was every bit as ruthless as Maxwell Black.

"I'm not going into rehab."

Maxwell didn't argue. He knew better.

Instead, he asked, "Have you considered how much your death from alcoholism-related disease will hurt your daughter?"

"She's an adult."

"Who would grieve your loss, with guilt she would never let go of. She's got a very tender heart."

"You don't have to tell me that." Grayson glared, fraying around the edges. "She's *my* daughter."

"Then you should know how your actions affect her."

"I'm not her responsibility. That's not how it works." But his words lacked conviction.

As well they should. Romi took care of her father and if he didn't see that, Grayson was being willfully blind.

"Are you saying you consider her yours?" he asked the older man.

"Yes, of course."

"Even though she's an adult?"

"Yes," the other man ground out.

"Then you owe her your sobriety."

"It's not that easy."

"Life never is."

"I miss her mother, damn it."

Maxwell *didn't* say that the older man spent too much of his time pickled with alcohol to miss anyone. Though he thought it. Or maybe it was the constant inebriation that made it impossible for the older Grayson to move on with his life.

His maudlin inability to move beyond his grief might well be fed by the alcoholism and not just vice versa.

But all Maxwell said was, "The deal depends on you going into rehab and staying until the doctor releases you."

"That's not going to happen." Grayson tossed the papers on his desk with a jerky movement. "There's not even a time limit."

"No, there isn't. You're staying until you have developed a new way to handle your grief."

"It's not just about grief. Not anymore," Grayson surprised Maxwell by admitting.

He'd known that, but he had not realized the older man was that self-aware.

"All the more reason to fix the problem now." Maxwell wasn't offering an out.

"It's not just a problem you can *fix*."

"I disagree."

"Then you go to rehab."

"I don't need it. You do." The man didn't need coddling.

He got enough of that and sweet understanding from his daughter. It was time for Harry Grayson to be the man Romi thought he was.

Grayson said with a lousy attempt at defiance, "I don't have to sign this contract."

"And I don't have to merge with your company. I can take it over without your cooperation. That's not what's at stake here."

"What is?"

"Visiting time with Romi."

"What the hell are you talking about?"

"You aren't going to keep hurting her. One way or another." Maxwell was under no illusion it would be easy to stage an intervention in Romi's life with her dad, but she was strong.

She would want Harry Grayson healthy more than her own comfort, no matter how much she might rather avoid the problem.

"She won't let you take her away from me." The words were strong, but the worried expression that accompanied them said Grayson wasn't as confident as they sounded.

"You underestimate my powers of persuasion." Maxwell, on the other hand, had no doubts about his own abilities.

"You underestimate her loyalty and strength of love."

"She won't be the one saying goodbye. *You* will."

Showing his brain still functioned, Grayson stopped arguing. "You'll do whatever you have to do to get your way."

"You know my reputation."

"I do. It's why your offer of a merger surprised me."

"Accept what I offer."

"Why? So you don't have to *take* what you want?"

"For Romi's sake."

The other man's face crumpled. "She's a good daughter."

"She deserves a healthy father."

"You must care about her or you wouldn't be pushing this."

Maxwell didn't know if Grayson was trying to convince himself or Maxwell, and he didn't care. He simply waited for the older man to agree to Maxwell's terms.

"Fine. I'll sign the contract. And the codicil."

"Good."

Maxwell made a call and his bodyguard and personal administrative assistant came in to witness the contract. As a licensed notary, his secondary assistant notarized the contract, too.

Cold-bloodedly efficient? Maybe.

But it worked for him.

"You're almost scarily resourceful."

Maxwell didn't deny it.

Grayson was cursing that truth fifteen minutes later when his bags were packed and Maxwell assigned him a bodyguard-babysitter that would make sure the other man would end up in the rehab center and stay there.

Romi breezed into the house at five minutes after noon, feeling anything but breezy.

But living by the mantra Never Let Them See You Sweat, she strove for nonchalance as she walked into the living room, where Mrs. K had told Romi she would find *Mr. Black* waiting for her.

His suit jacket removed and tossed over the back of a chair, his tie loosened and tailored slacks stretched attractively across his muscular thighs, Max relaxed on the sofa. The Grayson family photo albums covered the coffee table in front of him.

Max looked up from the one open in his lap. "Your mother was a beautiful woman."

"Yes, she was." Romi set her handbag down and crossed the room.

"You take after her." He offered her a view of the album that required she sit beside him to see it.

It would have been churlish to refuse, so she didn't. Tugging the hem of her tunic dress into place, Romi settled next to him. "Thank you, but most people think I look like my dad's side of the family."

"No." Maxwell gave a decisive shake of his head. "Your eyes are not only the same color as hers, but the same almond shape as well."

"She was a brunette." Romi's hair was the same color as her Grandmother Grayson's had been in her youth. Not that she'd ever met the family matriarch.

"You can see that it was the same fine texture. Like silk…" Max made the words a caress. "And it was straight like yours."

He grasped some strands of her hair between thumb and forefinger before sliding them down, maybe to show how *silky* her hair was?

For all the time Romi had spent studying the pictures of her mom, she'd never seen the things Max pointed out.

"I'm a shrimp compared to her." Four inches taller than her daughter, Jenna Grayson had been a willowy beauty.

"Same pixie-shaped face." He pointed to the pointed line of her mom's jaw. "See?"

Romi found herself nodding, caught by his sincerity.

"You also have the same way of holding your head when you are amused. Look at this picture, and this one." He grabbed one of the other albums.

"You really have been studying these. How long have you been waiting for me?" she asked, touched in a way she didn't want to admit.

Max set the album down and gave Romi a look she didn't understand, like he was trying to read something in her face. "Your father and I finished our business nearly two hours ago."

"And you waited all that time for me?"

"Yes."

"Why not leave and come back?" Or at least work on his table here? Why spend the time going through her family's photo history?

"I found enough to occupy myself."

He had, but certainly nothing she would have considered Maxwell Black spending his morning doing. It was just so *domestic*. And of all the words she'd used to describe this man, *domestic* was not one of them.

No matter how much he might care about his mother, she'd never thought of him as a *family* guy.

The strange intimacy of the moment getting to her, Romi stood up. "Let me just check in with my dad and then we can go to lunch." She didn't offer to change her clothes.

She'd worn a 1960s-inspired tunic dress in a bright pattern of yellow and white circles on a black background with leggings in the same shade of yellow when she left the house this morning. She'd had a strategy meeting with the local chapter of her favorite environmentalist group early that morning and then coffee with a woman instrumental in starting a series of successful charter schools around the country.

She couldn't believe her and Maddie's dream of starting their own charter school was so close to realization. Viktor Beck had offered to buy them a building as a wedding gift to Maddie.

Pretty wonderful, really.

Another reason Romi thought the guy might well be the right one for her best friend.

If her clothes were good enough for her meetings, they were good enough for Max.

She wasn't going to try to sex up the outfit.

Max stood as well. "Your father is not here."

"What?" He'd gone into the office? Today? "I thought—"

"You know we had a business discussion today."

"Yes."

"It went well."

"Good." She didn't have much else to add. "I don't really have much to do with Grayson Enterprises."

In case he didn't already realize that, but her dad had never once suggested Romi give up activism and her dream of running a charter school for the corporate world.

Max nodded, but he said, "I think in this instance, you will be interested in the outcome."

"Why?"

"Because it will affect you."

"I don't think so." Not in any way that really mattered.

Romi didn't have anything like the Madison family trust, but her Grandfather Grayson had left her enough money to help finance her dream of the school. She'd been shocked when the lawyers contacted her when she was a sophomore in college, but not too proud to take the money.

Even back then, she and Maddie had been talking dreams and Romi had known she needed money to get them off the ground.

Her dad had started his own trust for her on her birth.

She wasn't the heiress Maddie was, but Romi couldn't care less if her dad sold off his company. He didn't spend enough time there anymore for her to think it really mattered to him, either.

"I don't really care if he sells the business to you outright."

"Madison Beck cares what happens to Grayson Enterprises, very much in fact." Max's words came out in a warning tone.

"What?" Romi shook her head, but the words made no sense. "What in the world does that mean? Maddie doesn't care about business any more than I do."

"No, but she cares a great deal for you."

"I know that." They were sisters in everything but blood.

"And you care about her."

"You know I do."

Maxwell nodded his head, his pewter eyes reflecting both satisfaction and certainty. Or was that determination?

Whatever it was, it sent a frisson of something up Romi's spine. She couldn't call it fear because it felt way too much like anticipation.

Maddie always said Romi had an overdeveloped sense of adventure. Coming from Madcap Madison, the risk-taking heiress, that was saying something.

"Are you ready for lunch?" Max asked, as if he hadn't just been making cryptic comments latent with portent about her father's company and Romi's SBC.

"I think so?"

"Is that a question or a statement?" he prodded with some amusement.

"I'm not sure." In fact, she was fairly sure this lunch idea was a bad one, but she *had* come up with her deal and now was as good a time as any to proffer it to him. "You're an enigmatic guy, Max."

"And you wear your every thought on your lovely face."

"Opposites attract?"

His laughter was real and warm, a sound she knew very few ever heard. She treasured the moment despite her sense of confusion.

"Let's go. We will eat lunch."

"And talk." He'd said so.

"Yes."

"I have a deal for you," she offered, to show he wasn't the only one with plans for the future the other didn't know about.

"Do you?" he asked, still half-amused, but also clearly intrigued.

"Yep."

"You'll have to tell me about it in the car."

She considered talking about what she wanted to in the car. "Did you drive yourself?"

"Didn't you see the Maserati outside?"

"I wasn't really paying attention." She'd been thinking about what she was going to offer Max and practicing her nonchalance.

"I drove myself."

"Then we can talk in the car."

"So this deal has a private component?" he asked in a teasing tone.

She didn't hesitate to admit, "Very private."

"Interesting."

Here was hoping.

She'd noticed the other night that the Maserati was new, not the same car he'd had when they were dating before. More differences were apparent in the light of day.

His previous car had been luxurious, but this one was gorgeous and a little bigger. Was that just because it was a four-door?

"Please tell me you don't trade your cars as often as your bed partners."

He laughed as he pulled out of the circular drive in front of her home. "Not at all. I had my last car for five years before I bought this one."

"Wow, that's actually a long time. So, you are capable of longer-term commitment."

He didn't laugh like she expected. "A car is an investment, not a commitment."

So he still didn't like the *C* word. She wasn't surprised. "A sports car is an indulgence is what it is."

"The Maserati is an extremely well-made car."

"With impressive racing lines and an *über*-powerful engine." Even she was impressed by it.

He shrugged. "I don't mind the luxury, either."

"You'd be kinder to the environment if you drove a hybrid."

He actually shuddered. "No thank you."

She bit back laughter. "Many of the newer hybrids are more powerful than the earliest models."

"I will make you a deal, Romi."

"Yes."

"When Maserati designs a hybrid, I will buy it."

She smiled. "Deal."

"Until then, we'll settle for their foray into the more en-vironmentally conscious diesel engine."

"This is a diesel?"

"Yes."

"Hybrid would be better." Many environmentalists would actually disagree and she was sure he knew it, but she couldn't stop herself teasing him.

"Says you. We will have to agree to leave it up to you to drive the *greener* vehicles."

"I don't have a car at all."

"Your father's driver is at your disposal and if I am not mistaken, your father has a Daimler."

"I ride public transport most of the time. I only use Dad's car and driver when I have to dress up."

"What?" Max demanded, his tone sharp. "You ride pub-lic transport?"

"Yes." She grinned, feeling a little smug at his reaction.

"At night?" he asked with credible horror.

"Sometimes."

His jaw looked hewn from granite. "That is not safe."

"We aren't the Rockefeller branch of the Graysons, you know? Dad and I don't even have bodyguards."

Max swore. In Russian. It was kind of cute.

"Don't worry about it. San Francisco has a very confus-ing transportation system, but I've got it down. I know the fastest route everywhere I need to get in the city."

"You need a keeper." He didn't sound like he was joking.

"Are you applying for the job?"

He swore again. This time in English.

"Is that a *no?*" she pressed, really enjoying this more than she should be.

The sound that came out of his throat could have been a growl.

She giggled.

"Tell me about this deal you have for me," he instructed in a tight voice as they traversed familiar streets.

"I want you. That's no secret."

His nostrils flared, his eyes narrowing in shock. "No, it is not."

So, he hadn't been expecting this conversation, either. Nice. The Maxwell Blacks of the world could do with a little more of the unexpected in their lives. "And you want me."

"I do." Firm, unequivocal.

"Right. Only, I'm not interested in an affair."

"So you said a year ago."

Oh, she definitely had. And he'd listened.

Maybe it was the fact he *had* that made her capable of putting forth the offer she was about to. "But I'm also not particularly keen to remain a twenty-four-year-old virgin."

He flicked a quick glance at her, his expression now more than shocked. He didn't look superhappy with her pronouncement, either. "What do you plan to do about that?"

"That's what my deal is about."

"You want to make a deal for your virginity?" he demanded, sounding almost impressed.

"Not for, *about*. One night. You and me." He could read between the lines and get what she was offering.

"You want to have sex for one night?" he clarified, his voice strained.

"Yes."

"And then what?"

"And then we go our separate ways."

"Why only one night?"

"Because I don't want my heart broken." She just might survive a single night with him.

Any longer and she was going to be lost to love. How could she help it? Just looking at him told her he was her

ideal man, but she had the taste of pleasure from a year ago
to back that up.

"You are too honest for your own good."

"Am I?"

"Yes."

"You're not going to pretend that you didn't know I was
falling hard for you a year ago." She would be so disappointed if he tried to prevaricate on that point.

"No."

Good. "So, there wouldn't be any point in lying about it."

"No, I don't suppose there is." He turned on a familiar
street and she realized they weren't headed to any of his
usual haunts.

"So, what do you say?"

"To one night of sex?"

"Yes." Yikes, what else were they talking about?

"I say no."

"Good, so…" Her voice trailed off as his denial registered. "What? After all that…*are you kidding me?*"

He wanted her. She knew he did. He hadn't denied it,
either. What was wrong with him?

"I assure you, I would not joke about this."

"Well, why the heck not?"

"One night would be in direct conflict with my own
plans. I have my own deal for you to consider."

"What is it?" she asked with very little grace and even
less patience.

"Marriage."

She was still choking on her own breath in shock when
they turned into the parking garage for his apartment building.

CHAPTER FIVE

ROMI WAS STILL trying to come to terms with the bombshell Max had dropped in the car as he gave her a tour of his penthouse apartment.

She'd say he realized she needed time to collect herself, but that would be attributing a level of consideration she would never have accused him of in the past.

Not that he'd ever been *inconsiderate* with her, but he could change his name to Ruthless and it would so fit.

With a master suite that included a home office and a spa-sized bathroom, two guest bedrooms and a truly enormous living area that boasted a full-size living room, billiard area and dining room that merged into the kitchen, his home took up the entire top floor of his building.

Decorated in warm browns, coppers and brass accents, it was a very masculine space, but not at all utilitarian-feeling.

While the décor registered, his words sort of skated over her head. Her own thoughts were too scattered to settle in understanding, her hands cold and clammy where they were fisted at her sides.

Had he said *marriage* in the car?

Food was laid on the shiny mahogany table: small plates topped with Caesar salad, silver dome-covered entrée plates off to the side and a basket of Parmesan-crusted flatbread placed strategically between the two place settings. The tangy scent of Caesar dressing and garlic tickled her nose, even from the middle of the living room.

The setting was romantic, the Tiffany box on the table a glaring testament to the fact Max had *not* been joking in the car.

"Lunch smells good." She moved toward the table and then spun to face him, unable to hold it in any longer. *"You want to marry me?"*

"Now you react. I thought you might not have heard me." The humor in his tone was matched by the glint in his gorgeous gray eyes.

"I thought I had to have misheard you. Maybe you said *carriage*." It was as likely as what he actually had said. "Or *suffrage*, or *masonage*."

"Is that even a word?"

"Maybe? I don't know. The Masons are a real thing right, so *Masonage*." It should be a word.

In a move that would have appalled Helene Archer, who had been a free spirit in many ways, but firmly traditional when it came to proper manners, Romi rubbed her palms against the cotton knit of her leggings, getting rid of unwanted moisture.

His lips quirked at the corner. "I think perhaps you are in shock. Sit down. I will pour you a glass of wine."

"Shouldn't it be champagne?" she asked snarkily, but let him lead her to the table, where she settled into a chair with nothing like grace.

She just sort of plopped. Gobsmacked. That *was* a word, right? Kim from England, who had organized the clean air march back in April, said it sometimes.

Romi liked her. She was smart.

Oh, crap. Her mind was rabbiting all over the place to avoid that Tiffany box on the table.

"You don't want to marry me," she told him, sure she was right. "You don't want to get married at all."

"You are mistaken."

Finally, something other than total annihilating confusion pushed at Romi's brain. Anger suffused her. "A year ago, you were pretty clear that you weren't looking for a lifetime."

"No one can promise that." Oh, he sounded so superior.

"You are wrong, Max. I know that's hard for you to comprehend, but in this? You are totally off-base." She crossed her arms and glared up at all six feet five inches of him. "Millions of people make just those kinds of promises all the time."

He wasn't impressed. The flat line of his lips and equally flat look in his pewter eyes told her that. "And break them as often as not."

"They still make them." And if Max made a promise?

He would keep it. Ruthless he might be, but he kept his word. It was why he didn't give it very often.

"That meeting I attended with Madison and her father was very illuminating," Max said, apropos of nothing.

Romi continued to glare at him, letting her annoyance show. "Are you determined to keep me off balance?"

"It is a good negotiation tactic."

"Am I a competitor you are hoping to *absorb* or *defeat*?" she asked, sounding downright cranky.

Which she was on the verge of being. So, okay. Yeah. Really irritated. He was talking about marriage like it was a business deal and that was just a really raw wound right now, after everything Maddie had been through lately.

"No, you are the woman I intend to marry."

"You aren't making any sense. You do know that, right?" Seriously. He had to know it.

"I am speaking English."

"Mostly. You did curse in Russian."

He shrugged and she didn't belabor the point. She was getting side-tracked again and even she knew she needed to rein in her wayward thoughts.

"You don't love me." That was something she was very sure of.

He almost looked regretful. "Love is not in my emotional repertoire."

"Tell your mom that."

"Familial love is not the same as romantic love as you are well aware."

This man! He would test the patience of Santa Claus and Romi was no children's benevolent holiday trope. "They come from the same place."

"So you say."

She rolled her eyes. "Pretty much everyone agrees that love—all kinds of love—comes from the heart."

"My heart beats blood, not bloody-minded emotion." Spoken with his typical certainty, the claim focused on the concrete rather than the concept.

"You're being obtuse on purpose."

"No." Oh, he just oozed sincerity and certainty. "We simply do not agree on this point."

"When I marry it will be to a man who loves me as much as my father loved my mother." Of that she was very sure.

She settled her once cold, now shaking, hands in her lap, unwilling to admit how much she'd hoped that might be him at one time.

Max looked supremely unconvinced. "I have no desire to be a carbon copy of your father."

"He's not weak." That's not what Max had said, but she knew what he meant.

"He is, but he is also intelligent, loyal and willing to dig for the inner strength he has not utilized in too long."

"Wow, I don't know what to say to that." She was all set to just be mad at this man and then he showed so much humanity, she couldn't ignore it.

"Say you will hear me out, with an open mind."

She sighed, wishing this conversation could actually go somewhere meaningful. "Some things are not negotiable, Max."

Leaning toward her, he cupped her cheeks with gentle

firmness. "And sometimes we are surprised by the compromises we are willing to make."

She wanted to say his touch made her weak, but what it really did was make her feel things that made her doubt her own convictions. Was that just another definition of weakness? Or something more?

"This marriage idea is a compromise for you." He desired her enough to offer it and that blew her mind really, but that kind of physical passion without love was just lust.

And lust made a lousy basis for a marriage. The divorce rate and tabloid headlines made that reality clear pretty much every day.

"My dad did not offer you part of Grayson Enterprises to marry me." She knew that without a doubt.

"No, but his company is involved."

She moved her head away from that too-inspiring touch and he let her go.

"How?" she asked.

"Did Madison tell you her father threatened your father's company in order to try to force her into Jeremy's plans for her marriage?"

"Maddie married Viktor to save my dad's company?" Romi asked, feeling like all the air was slowly being sucked from the room.

"Oh, no. Your sister-by-choice is a formidable opponent." Max's admiration was clear.

Regardless of the very unfamiliar sting of jealousy, particularly directed at her SBC, Romi said, "Maddie is amazing."

"She gave your father a very limited opportunity to take the threat off the table."

"But he didn't." Romi knew Jeremy Archer well enough to guess that.

"No."

"What did Maddie do?" If she hadn't given in to her dad's bullying, she'd done something big to make him back off.

"Madison told Archer that if your father's company was under threat on her twenty-fifth birthday, all of the shares to AIH in her trust fund would be transferred to your father personally."

"What? No. She can't do that!"

"I assure you it has been done. She signed the paperwork that afternoon."

"How do you know?"

"Do you really need to ask?"

No. If this man wanted information, he would get it. "But you're going into business with my father. Even AIH can't touch him."

"Our contract is written in such a way that his company will be under threat by *me* if certain conditions are not met." He didn't sound triumphant *or* guilty. Just matter-of-fact.

"What conditions?"

"Do you really want details? Suffice to say, measurables over which I will have full control for the next six months."

"You wouldn't manipulate things so my dad lost his company. You just wouldn't." That was so…ruthless.

Oh, man. He *would* do it because this man had a ruthless streak about as wide as the Golden Gate Bridge.

"I don't plan to, no. I *intend* to rebuild your father's company and use it as a springboard for other things." No modesty in that statement.

"Provided I go along with your *deal*."

Max nodded, no ambivalence about that reality evident in his manner. "That is part of it, yes."

"What is the other part?"

"Your father in rehab."

"What? How?" She'd tried, but it was too hard.

Too hard to hold her dad accountable, too hard to push when she was better at avoidance and she loved him so much.

She'd change the world, but it wouldn't start at home.

"It's part of our contract. However, although your father

has signed everything and is as we speak on his way to a very exclusive, very discreet rehabilitation facility with a success rate of over seventy percent, I haven't signed the contract yet."

"And you won't if I don't marry you?" She could barely believe the mercenary tactic. "How could you hold his health hostage like that? That's monstrous, Max. You have to know that."

"You forget, I'm holding his company, too."

"I don't care."

"I realized that."

"So, you adjusted your plans accordingly." The man *was* a monster.

But he *wasn't*. Darn it. She knew Max better than that. He *was* ruthless and pragmatic to the point of emotionlessness about some things.

But he wasn't a monster.

Just a very determined shark who didn't mind getting some blood in the water if that meant feasting.

"What are the terms of the marriage?" There had to be some.

A man like Maxwell Black didn't make this kind of offer without covering all the contingencies.

"The usual terms, I would imagine, with a well-structured prenuptial agreement."

"Because you don't anticipate it lasting."

"No." Brutal honesty.

But then, could she expect anything else with this man?

"Is there an expiration date?" she asked.

"Not exactly."

"What does that mean?" A year ago, he'd had a very definitive end date in mind for their affair.

"Either of us can end the marriage at any time."

"But there will be consequences as laid out in the prenup?"

"Naturally."

"For both of us." She didn't know why she was so sure of that, particularly considering the conversation so far, but she was.

"Absolutely."

"Why, Max?"

"Because contrary to your unexpected and rather inexplicable offer, you don't believe in uncommitted sex." He began to eat like their discussion was no more earth-shattering than planning a follow-on date.

Maybe for him, it wasn't.

Only she didn't believe that, either.

She pulled some of her earlier nonchalance around her as she began to eat as well. He didn't have to know it was a facade over roiling emotions and cacophonous thought. "As you said, people change."

"No, I said circumstances change. It takes a lot more to change people."

"How can you be so smart about some stuff and so ignorant about other things?" she wondered aloud, not even really asking him, just astonished by the reality.

"What am I ignorant about?"

"Love."

"The refusal to succumb is not ignorance, it is an informed decision." Max sighed, sounding as close to tired as she'd ever heard him. "You know I don't believe in forever, this gives you the trappings of commitment you need."

"With an out clause for you."

"Since divorce law in this country allows the eventual dissolution of any marriage so long as the party seeking dissolution is committed to her course, that is already an out clause."

For the most part, that was true. "You must have a time line you believe our so-called marriage will fall into."

"There will be nothing *so-called* about it. You will be mine, Romi. Make no mistake. And I will be yours in every way the law dictates."

"You sound like a caveman right now." And she liked it. Way too much. "Or a throwback tsar."

"Sue me."

She almost laughed, but couldn't quite release the tension. "How long?"

"Until?"

"The sell-by date."

"That is crass."

"The *time line* then."

"Most negative repercussions outlined in the prenup are nullified at the ten-year mark."

"Ten years?"

"Is practically a lifetime."

"Not even close." But married to someone incapable of love? She very much feared he would be right.

"So, let me get this straight. You want sex with me?"

"Yes."

"And you're willing to blackmail me into marrying you?"

He offered her a piece of flatbread. "Yes."

"No complaint about the terminology." She accepted the bread, a sense of unreality surrounding her.

He shrugged. "Much of business is done in the same way. Terms don't change realities."

"I offered you a night of sex." And he'd turned her down.

"I want more than a night."

Right. "You want ten years."

"Maybe more."

"And maybe less."

"You may be ready to walk away before I am." He didn't sound concerned about that, but he also didn't sound like they were just words to placate.

Idiot. Really. Mr. Brilliant Businessman-Corporate Tsar had no clue.

"But fidelity until divorce?" she asked, that sense of unreality nearly drowning her.

"Nonnegotiable."

"What about children?"

"Children?" he asked, like he'd never heard the word before.

"You know, the little people that call you dad."

"Papa. Russian children call their fathers *papa*."

It was such a curious mix, the bits of his heritage he refused to let go and the elements to his character and life that were purely American.

"Well, do you want any babies that will grow up to call you papa?"

He went completely still, a bite partway to his mouth. She wasn't even sure he was still breathing. His expression was indescribable, but something about what she'd said had struck a chord deep inside him.

"My mother would like a grandchild." The words did not match the awed tone in his voice.

He resumed eating, but she wasn't fooled. He was no more nonchalant about this conversation than she was, if for very different reasons. Or maybe just fewer reasons. The idea of having his children unraveled something inside her.

"What about *you?* Would *you* like a child?" she pressed.

A new emotion flickered in Maxwell's gray eyes. Yearning. "Yes. I would like a child."

"Would having a child change the sell-by date on the marriage?" She wanted to know.

"People with children divorce all the time."

That was not what she'd wanted to hear, true as it might be. "Would you want to see your child only a couple of weekends a month?"

"We would share custody." But he didn't sound any more enthusiastic about that prospect than she felt.

Romi narrowed her eyes and challenged, "Would we?"

"Perhaps we should consider remaining married until our child goes to college."

"What if we have more than one?"

"Would you want to?" The awe was there again.

And it touched her when she wanted very much to keep her wits about her. "I'd always hoped to have more than one child." Hardly a secret, it wasn't hard to admit. "I would have loved to have a sibling that actually lived with me."

"As opposed to your sister-by-choice."

"You don't know how many times I wished Maddie had been my sister by birth. We agreed a long time ago we wanted more than one child because we wanted something different for our own families."

"How many children do you want?" he asked cautiously.

"At least two, maybe more." She shared Maddie's dream of possibly adopting at some point.

Max didn't look upset by her answer. Far from it, he appeared intrigued. "Russians put a premium on family."

"And yours was truncated."

"Exactly."

"So, you are saying you want more than one child." From the man who *still* considered *commitment* a dirty word, despite his claim he wanted to marry her.

For him, a wedding really was just a piece of paper—a contract that could be adhered to, or broken with consequences.

Even so...

"This conversation is beyond surreal," she said helplessly. Surely he could see that.

"I do not agree. It is the conversation we should have had a year ago, I think." He laid his silverware on his plate, clearly done with his salad.

"Are you kidding me? After a few dates?" Put that way, it didn't make a whole lot more sense *now*.

"I knew I wanted you. You made your terms clear."

"I wasn't negotiating terms when we broke up." Was it a breakup when the number of dates wouldn't count all the fingers on one hand?

"Nevertheless, you revealed what it would take to get you into my bed."

"I *revealed* that on the way over here."

His brows rose, his disbelief clear. "Do you honestly believe one night would be enough for us?"

"That's not the point."

"What is the point?"

He wanted honesty? She'd give him some truth. "The whole point of one night is because no *limited* time would ever be enough. I was falling for you a year ago and my heart doesn't have very far to go before we hit the place of no return. I do not want to fall in love with a man who considers it a weakness, can't you understand that?"

"Are you so sure you have a choice?"

Crap. That hurt. She gasped with a real live physical pain as the truth of *his* words sank in.

Nevertheless, she wasn't taking that lying down. "I think you don't have a lot to say about an emotion you refuse to feel."

"We are different people, Romi."

"No kidding."

Rather than annoying him, her sarcasm made him smile. And that irritated *her*.

"You wear your heart on your sleeve."

"At least I have a heart," she retorted, stung.

"Yes, you do. A generous one."

"How can you sound so admiring when you've made it clear it's a trait you don't actually admire?"

"I never said I found your ability to love a weakness."

"But for you it would be?" she asked, confused.

"As I said, we are different people. You are willing to risk the pain of eventual separation for the benefit of the temporary emotion."

"What if it isn't temporary? What if it never goes away?" That was what scared her the most with him.

Maxwell Black could end up being her one true love. As cheesy as some might consider that, Romi believed in soul mates. Her parents had been.

And while Romi wanted nothing more than to have that kind of love for herself, she did not want to spend the rest of her life grieving for a lost love. Particularly one who had simply walked away.

"There is no actual expiration on the marriage," he pointed out. "Read the contract."

"No, because it's not what you have on paper that worries me. It's what is going on inside *you*, Max. You expect to get bored eventually. You expect to walk away."

"No."

"But, you said—"

"I acknowledge the *probability* that our marriage will not last. I do not demand that it end at some point."

Which was actually a huge departure from his attitude the year before. "I just don't understand what you hope to get out of this."

"Your body."

All the air really left the room this time, Romi's vision going black around the edges.

With a muttered Russian imprecation, Max jumped up and then he was there, holding her so she would not slide sideways out of her chair.

Her fuzzy gaze settled on the Tiffany ring box. *That* did not help her sense of disorientation.

"You need to finish eating. We will continue this discussion after you have done so."

"You think I'm suffering low blood sugar?" she asked with a near hysterical laugh.

First of all, she was almost finished with her salad—even if it had been appetizer-sized—and a piece of flatbread. Second of all, his words were the problem. Not the food, or the fact she hadn't eaten all of it.

"You are suffering something. Now, eat." He removed the dome covering her plate and traded it for the salad plate before going around the table to do the same for his own lunch.

Certain she couldn't eat any more, half of Romi's artichoke-and-egg-white quiche and its accompanying slice of melon was gone before she realized she was wrong.

She stared across the table at Max, unaccountably cranky that he might have been right. Sometimes she needed protein and the fact he'd taken note of that during their brief time together made her feel strange.

That didn't make the topic of their conversation any more normal, either. "So, if I don't marry you, you're going to take my father's company, thereby triggering Maddie's crazy fail-safe and just in case that's not enough, you'll revoke your support of my dad going into rehab?"

Repeating it didn't make the threat any less outrageous than when he'd made it, or any easier to understand.

Max didn't even flicker an eyelid. "Yes."

"What does that make you?"

"The winner."

CHAPTER SIX

"Is THAT ALL that matters to you?" she asked with shock, when really, she had no reason to be surprised. She made no effort to hide her unease with the idea. "That you win?"

"I *never* go into a fight without the intention of doing just that and the certainty I can do so."

"Have you ever lost?" she wondered out loud.

"I lost my Russian family before I knew what it meant to have anyone in my life besides my mother."

"That wasn't your fight. It was your mom's." And while the loss was very real, and no doubt impacting, even to an emotionless tycoon who relegated marriage to a business deal, it wasn't an example of Max being defeated.

"She won her independence and the life she wanted for me at great cost. Mama still misses her family."

"So, you were raised not to count the cost, but to weigh the victory." It was the attitude of strength, one that made no allowance for fear.

She was impressed despite herself.

"That is a very good way to put it." He smiled. "Mama would be proud."

"Don't think I haven't noticed that you didn't answer my question." One thing a professional at avoidance like Romi could do was recognize the tactic.

"I have never come out the loser in a business deal."

No doubt, but that wasn't exactly what she was asking. Since Romi didn't actually see marriage as a business deal.

"What about personally?" Though she couldn't imagine him really fighting for anything on a personal basis.

Before today anyway.

He certainly hadn't fought to keep seeing her a year ago. She'd told him no and he'd accepted her word without trying to change her mind. She'd vacillated between relief and disappointment.

The relief had been unwarranted emotion, she now realized. Maxwell Black didn't give up. He just regrouped.

"Not since I became an adult."

"Your mom's family does not count, we've already said."

"Every loss counts," he responded implacably.

And he said he had no heart. For the first time since meeting him, Romi wondered if the heart he claimed not to be guided by was just buried *really* deep.

"Then you shouldn't have any trouble remembering them."

Rather than answer, he stood and indicated the living room with a tip of his head. "Would you like to move this discussion somewhere more comfortable?"

They ended up side by side on the big brown leather sectional even though there were several seating options that would not have required such close proximity.

He settled back into the corner, his arm along the back, his gaze holding hers. "Despite having a relationship with my mother that lasted more than two years, my father walked away from me without a backward glance."

"You don't know that." She kicked her ballet flats off and tucked one foot under her, turning to face him more squarely.

"I do."

"Have you spoken to him?" She tried to picture that conversation and couldn't quite do it.

"No."

"Then you don't know what regrets are still open wounds

in his heart." She could not fathom any parent *not* regretting being a nonentity in Max's life.

Ruthless the man might be, but he was a son to be proud of.

"He offered money and bringing his influence to bear to facilitate our immigration in exchange for silence on my mother's part. Both about her relationship with him and about my existence. She was never even allowed to name him."

"That could be because his choices were limited, not because he didn't want you." She didn't know why it was so important to her to convince Max of that.

"Your heart is too tender." He reached out to brush her hair behind her ear. "You need someone to watch over you and make sure the world does not rip it to shreds."

"Like you're trying to do?"

He let his hand fall away. "Not even close. I'm offering you a place in my life, not coming after you with a scalpel directed at your heart."

"Nice image." No way was she going to admit she missed the warmth of his hand.

"I am Russian. Imagery is in my blood."

"Russians are also known for their passionate natures."

"You have reason to believe that of me." His meaning was clear.

He was equating passion to sex while she'd been talking about emotion. Nothing new about that, but maybe it wasn't the epic misunderstanding she'd always considered it.

He was willing to acknowledge his sexual nature and need. Could that be a way to his heart?

And did she have the courage to even try?

Did she even want to? Was the remote possibility of finding a way to his deeper emotions worth putting hers at risk?

She could walk away right now and it would hurt, but she would get over him.

Eventually.

The past year had at least shown her the former if not the latter.

But he wasn't just asking her to take a chance on dating, on a relationship. He wasn't *asking* anything.

He was blackmailing her and because Max saw the whole thing as some kind of business deal with fringe benefits, he didn't even think there was anything wrong with that.

"The fringe benefits, as you call them, go both directions," he said, a sardonic twist to his mouth.

"I said that out loud, didn't I?" Darn it.

He smirked, his hand gliding along her thigh suggestively. "Yes."

Romi did her best to ignore the sparks dancing along her nerve endings from his touch. "So, you're not going to tell me about the loss that proved to you that love was weakness, are you?"

"You believe I've suffered some trauma that left me incapable of letting my emotions control me?" He left his hand resting on her thigh, but stilled its movement.

"Have you?"

"I learned early that romantic love didn't count for much when other more important considerations were on the table, but it wasn't anything my mother hadn't been telling me since before I could walk."

Romi couldn't take her eyes off that large masculine hand covering her thigh. "Your mom doesn't believe in love?"

"With good reason. No affection ever lasted beyond the point at which she became an inconvenience."

"She doesn't seem bitter." While Romi had only met her a handful of times, she'd never gotten the impression that Natalya Black was one of those cynical women that made everyone bleed with their bitterness.

"She is not. She is a realist."

Who had taught her son to see erotic love as a weakness. "And she wanted to protect you from heartache."

"Yes." He looked a little surprised by the idea and his own agreement to it.

"How old were you when you learned this lesson?" The idea of him in love hurt her in some indefinable way, especially if he'd been a vulnerable teen, risking his heart.

"Ten."

"So not a personal loss?" Surprise, surprise.

"It was very personal."

"But the romance was between your mother and her lover." No way had Max been in love at such a young age.

"*Batya* made Mama glow for three years."

"He was Russian?"

"No. He was American. *Batya* is a Russian nickname for father. It is what I called him."

And Max hadn't reverted to using the man's given name later. That said something about how deeply the hurt went. How ingrained that role had been in Max's heart.

"And you?"

"He lived with us, though I realized later it must only have seemed that way. Our home was not his, but he was *there* every evening, adding a sense of security to our small house. *Batya* took me to ball games, came to my school and culture center activities. He sat at the head of our table on holidays and took us out for our birthdays."

In other words, he'd *been* Max's dad. For a little while anyway. "But it didn't last."

"No."

"Why?"

"Does it matter?"

"Probably not." The lesson here was that Max had clearly opened his heart to this man who had acted like a father, only to have it crushed when the man walked away.

"Have you ever been in love?"

"No chance." The words were spoken with such quiet vehemence, she knew he had never been that vulnerable teenager she worried about.

Max truly had learned his lessons early and he'd taken them to heart until no one would accuse him of having one.

"Me, either." And honestly?

She wasn't keen to fall right now, but every minute spent in this man's company was undermining Romi's belief she had any say in the matter.

She wasn't sure what it was about that sad little story that got to her so much, but no way could she ever see Max as a monster. No matter what pressures he brought to bear for his marriage plan.

"You really hedged your bets with this marriage thing, didn't you?" she asked, needing to move away from the emotional morass their discussion had become for her.

"If by that you mean I considered every contingency, you would be right."

"Maddie is out of town on her honeymoon. You know I don't want to interrupt her with a call to ask about her contingency plan."

"You do not trust me regarding the details?"

"Should I?"

He considered that for a moment. "Perhaps not, but I have never lied to you, nor will I ever."

"I'm not sure you telling me that in the same conversation you admit to setting up a truly untenable situation for me can carry much weight for me."

Max's eyes narrowed. "Call Jeremy Archer."

"He lies."

"If anything, he would be tempted to deny it, yes?"

"Yes. So, why would *you* trust him to back you up?"

Max shrugged. "Few businessmen in this town would cross me without very strong provocation. Viktor maybe, but Jeremy? He's too wrapped up in his company to risk it by lying about me."

"Without compelling cause."

"Precisely."

"How do I know my dad is in rehab?" She wasn't sure

what was pushing her to question the reliability of everything he claimed, but she had this irresistible urge to prick the bubble of his confidence.

Even if only a little.

Rather than appear in the list "pricked," Max looked smugly satisfied by his planning. "He will get a single phone call before going into immersion therapy, during which he will be allowed no external contact. Not with family. Not for his business."

"That works in your favor."

"It is my habit to make sure most things do."

"Wow, the arrogance level just skyrocketed in here."

Max smiled, amusement glinting in his gray eyes. "Arrogance is defined as excessive confidence. Mine, on the other hand, is well-founded."

"I won't argue that."

"I would not expect you to. You are far too intelligent to take on the hopeless cause."

"Oh, I don't know. According to a lot of men in your position, my activism on behalf of the environment is exactly that."

"I do not agree."

And that should give her hope, shouldn't it? How pragmatic was it to be a CEO so committed to sustainability? She was sure he would say very pragmatic, but only if you had an eye and a *heart* for the future.

Was he closer? He seemed closer. "Tell me something."

"Anything." The heat of his hand burned through the fabric of her leggings.

"I wish you meant that, but I won't push it." The temptation to lean into him was huge and growing. She fought it, trying to stay focused on what needed saying. "I just need confirmation of something."

"Yes?"

"Would you ever walk away from your child as your father and your mother's lover did with you?"

"No." The word fell with the weight of a boulder between them, every ounce of lust in his expression transforming to determination.

No doubt he meant it.

It made her doubt his willingness to walk away from her as well. He thought he could and most likely would, but she wasn't so sure. Especially if they decided to have children together.

If he didn't let himself love her, he wasn't going to fall for someone else, either. And no other power but love was going to make this man rip the fabric of his family.

No matter what he told himself, or her, for that matter.

"You are just a mass of contradictions, aren't you?"

"Not at all," he said with a different kind of force and obvious horror at the very idea.

She laid down her own line in the sand. "I'm not agreeing to anything today." She waited for him to take that in.

If his first reaction was to try to obliterate it, they were done here. No matter what extra aces he'd slipped into his hand, she wasn't playing.

"Today?" he asked with emphasis on the single word.

"Today."

"This is not an indefinite offer."

"Oh, I know, but you're smart enough to realize that little box isn't getting opened this afternoon." She flicked her head toward the dining table and the Tiffany box still sitting unopened near her now empty plate.

Max's head tilted, a predatory light growing in his eyes. "I thought it was."

"Well, I guess even Corporate Tsars can be wrong sometimes."

"Perhaps." Nothing in his expression or relaxed posture indicated that bothered him.

He seemed…well, turned on. And that wasn't what she was expecting in reaction to her statement. Though it certainly didn't hurt in regard to how she wanted to spend the rest of their afternoon.

"Tonight, today…whatever, we go with *my* plan."

"That entails…?" he asked with the air of a man who already knew.

Maybe he did. Or maybe, he was just so good at exuding confidence, it came naturally—even when he was in the dark.

"You and I test out our sexual compatibility in a bed and with complete follow-through." He had to know what that meant because she wasn't spelling it out. "I talk to my dad when he calls. Tomorrow, I talk to Jeremy Archer. Depending on that conversation, I decide whether I need to interrupt my SBC's honeymoon."

"You will not." Max sounded so sure of that fact.

But then, as Romi had already acknowledged, he always did. Uncertainty wasn't in Max's repertoire any more than love was. Since calling Maddie was on the very bottom of the list of things Romi wanted to do right now, she wasn't going to argue regardless.

"Tomorrow night, I eat dinner alone. I think about what you are offering and what you are threatening and if I can reconcile the two."

Or if she could live with the consequences of not doing so. Romi was pretty sure that didn't need saying.

Apparently Max agreed with her, because he merely nodded. "We will have lunch again the day after."

"You can bring your little blue box. It will either get opened, or not."

He shifted so he was very much in her personal space, his body surrounding hers as one arm slid around her waist and the one on the back of the couch moved to rest behind her head. "You show very little curiosity regarding a piece of jewelry you will be wearing for some time to come."

"Jewelry isn't going to sway me." But his nearness might.

"No more than the salvation of your father's company."

"Right." But the salvation of her father?

That was something else entirely. It was everything. And Max had set it in motion, no matter what his supposed motivations for doing so were.

"You're taking this delay really well," she breathed, his face almost close enough to kiss. Realization came over her slowly. "You knew I would ask for time."

"I had hoped you would make a quick decision, but I was prepared to give a week." However, he had expected her to open the ring box.

He would learn that for all the trappings of wealth that surrounded her, Romi wasn't all that interested in them.

"And I only asked for three days."

"A decent compromise."

She almost laughed at the idea of Maxwell Black compromising with anyone, but the truth was that he considered the entire marriage idea a compromise. And he *had* allowed a counteroffer.

For time at least.

Max hadn't said no about the sex. From the way he was sitting and the alpha male pheromones saturating the air around them, she didn't think he was going to, either.

Romi wasn't sure why that was so important, but it was. She needed to link with him intimately before making a decision.

At this point, she wasn't looking for logic or reason. Romi's instincts were telling her she needed the physical connection and she wasn't going to ignore them.

Maxwell did not need convincing when it came to giving in to Romi's desire to give herself to him fully.

No, she clearly did *not* see it that way, but she had never allowed another man the same level of intimacy.

Maxwell could not figure out why she was offering the gift to him now, without things settled between them. But then, that was no new situation for him with her. Her mind worked in ways his did not.

Perhaps it was as simple as her needing a sense of some control over the situation.

He wasn't averse to giving her that.

Was in fact ridiculously eager to do so. It was just that she had looked so damn vulnerable when she'd found out about her father's rehab.

Maxwell had not cared for the feeling that he was doing something wrong. He knew he was not.

Maxwell had not put Madison's shares up for grabs as a bargaining tool. His willingness to use that situation did not make him a villain. It made him smart.

And *he* had not led Harry Grayson down the path of functioning alcoholism. Maxwell had in fact convinced the older man to go somewhere he could get help with his addiction.

Was he willing to follow through on his threat to back out of the deal? Yes.

Had Maxwell ever considered, even for a moment, it would come to that? No.

He wasn't the monster Romi seemed to think him.

No matter what she might think, Maxwell wanted her to accept the terms of his deal, not simply give in to them.

If his successful years in business had taught him one thing, it was that voluntary partners worked harder to make the venture work. It wasn't always a luxury he could afford himself, but when possible, Maxwell maneuvered his rivals into wanting the mergers he chose to pursue.

Something niggled at considering his marriage proposal just another business merger, but that was essentially exactly what it was. Right?

Pushing aside the uncomfortable thoughts, he considered his next move. No question it involved making love to Romi, but did he start here and take her to the bedroom?

Considering his hair trigger where she was concerned,

if they began here—even with the most basic of kisses—chances were, this is where Romi would gift him her virginity.

She deserved more ceremony than that.

He would take her to his bed, not the guest room where he conducted most of his sexual trysts. His wrought-iron bed, imported from the ironmasters in Russia, had never been occupied by anyone but him.

Using more control than he realized would be necessary, he pulled away from the allure of her body and stood. Maxwell put his hand out to Romi. "Come, we will have your sexual taste test."

She burst out laughing, all traces of the overly emotional, dangerously vulnerable woman drowning under her sweet humor. "That is not what I said."

"But it is what you meant?"

"Maybe I'm just ready to lose my virginity."

"Maybe there is something going on here *neither* of us understands." He liked that idea much better than him being the only one in the dark.

"Oooh, the Corporate Tsar doesn't know everything. How disconcerting that must be for you."

"I am used to that unfortunate turn of events around you."

"I confuse you?" she asked, sounding really far too happy about the possibility.

"Do you doubt it? Have we not established that we are very different people?"

"You're nothing like Jeremy Archer, or my dad for that matter, but you understand them. Don't try to pretend you don't."

"You, Romi, are an enigma."

She preened. "Well, that's nice to know."

He shook his head. "Like right now. I do not understand why this is so satisfying *and* amusing to you."

"You are a very dangerous man to me, Maxwell Black,"

she said with a lot more serious mien than she had shown only a second before. "It's good to know you don't have it all easy with me."

"I would call you anything but easy, *milaya*."

Her blue gaze sparked with heat as she placed her hand in his and stood. "You know I love when you use Russian endearments."

He *did* know it. Though once again, he was not sure he understood why. But it was easier to use Russian endearments than English for him.

His mother had never used the English terms and while he would admit it aloud only under the threat of his company's dissolution, Russian was the language of what passed for his heart.

Unlike her silent and rather bemused response to his tour earlier, Romi commented on the décor on the way to his bedroom, seemingly surprised it felt like a home rather than a hotel room.

"Why would my home feel like a hotel?" he had to ask.

"Well, because decorators often go generic when they do places for men like you."

"Men like me?" He pressed against the door to his study with his back, pushing it open wide enough for them to enter.

"Corporate Tsars," she said with the tiniest bit of sarcasm lacing the second word.

Her allusion to his royal attitude was not lost on Maxwell, but he refused to pretend to be other than what he was. A man who knew what he wanted and had a decided talent for figuring out how to get it.

"If I wanted to live in a place that looked like a hotel, I would live in one." If he wanted to live in a palace, he'd live in one of those, too.

"See, that's the way I always thought. You should have heard me and Maddie when Jeremy had his mansion re-decorated."

"It is not the warmest of abodes." There was nothing wrong with the mansion if you wanted to live in luxury without personality.

The designer who had redone the Archer house had obviously been very knowledgeable in his or her field—talented even—but it was a cold place with no evidence a family lived there.

Though Maxwell supposed with just Jeremy Archer in residence, a *family* didn't. "It's a showplace for a megarich tycoon who likes to impress and intimidate with his surroundings as much as his money."

Maxwell's own strategy for how his home came across to visitors was more subtle. His penthouse reflected him and his wealth in a way that let others know he was not afraid for them to know who he was.

Of course, that was because nothing of manipulative value could be discovered visiting the main areas of his home. His favorite colors? His preference for dark wood? Yes.

Even his Russian heritage and wholesale acceptance of the country of his second citizenship, America.

What no one saw, unless they were looking very closely and knew how to read such things—not a common occurrence—was his desire for control or his genuine affection for his mother.

There was only a single formal picture of her in the living area. His bedroom suite was different.

There, much of what made Maxwell the man he was could be seen on display.

Hence the dearth of invitations to that sanctum.

He did not invite women to the bed in which he slept for a reason. The only friend who had been in his personal office in memory was Viktor Beck, and the only people who had seen every room in his apartment were his mother and his cleaning staff.

Before today.

Today, Maxwell brought Romi into his private sanctuary without hesitation.

She seemed to realize the enormity of it when they stepped over the threshold into his office. She stopped and drew in a shocked breath. "You are in here."

"I am indeed."

"No, I know." She rolled her eyes. "You're so droll. I mean, I can see *you* in this room. I thought your apartment was so much *your* home, but this? This is like a glimpse at your heart."

"You are assuming on that heart thing again."

She shook her head, not even cracking a smile. "Thank you for bringing me here."

"It was part of your deal."

"No, sex was my deal. That could have happened in a guest room."

He winced.

Her eyes narrowed. "That's where you take your lovers, isn't it?"

He shrugged. She'd guessed. There was no point in confirming it.

"You know if I do marry you, we'll be buying *all* new furniture for those rooms, right?"

"Whatever you want."

"I'm pretty sure that's not how things work with you. I may not have gotten the full meal, but the taste I had was not a man who gave his partner whatever she wanted."

"On the contrary, I am very good at determining what it is you *really* want and giving it."

"You were a year ago, that's for sure." Her blue eyes glowed with remembered passion.

CHAPTER SEVEN

ROMI GAZED AT him with nothing less than adoration. "Other men aren't like you."

"You tested this theory?" Maxwell demanded even as he basked unashamedly in her evident approval of his sexual prowess.

"You know I didn't."

"Then how do you know?"

She blushed. "I just do."

He found her innocence charming when the same in other women had acted as a huge red flag for Maxwell.

He stopped in the middle of his office, and brushed his hand along her heated cheek. "Yes, but how, sweet little Romi?"

"I may be a virgin, but that doesn't mean I've never done anything with other guys."

"Like?" he pressed, wondering if she realized they were engaged in foreplay.

She rolled her expressive eyes. "I've kissed other men."

"And on the basis of kissing alone..." He leaned down and pressed his lips to hers, taking advantage of her surprised gasp for a small taste before lifting his head. "You have determined I am unique?"

She blinked up at him.

He smiled.

"You're starting now, aren't you?" she asked.

"I began in the living room."

She looked like she was realigning her thoughts based on his claim and then she nodded. "Like I said. No one like you."

"Did you do more than kiss with other men?" he asked, allowing his breath to caress her lips.

Her pupils dilated, her expression going dreamy. "Hmmm?"

"Other men," he reminded her. "Your experience with them."

"Some touching."

"Here?" he asked, brushing along her back.

"What? I don't…" She swayed toward him. "Maybe? I think so."

He liked this proof she could not think clearly from the simple touches. His own libido was already in overdrive.

"What about here?" he asked as he cupped her nape and ran his thumb down to her pulse point.

She moaned, leaning into a kiss he kept brief by necessity. They *would* make it to the bedroom.

"No one ever took over like you do." Her words weren't an answer to his teasing.

But they were exactly what Maxwell wanted to hear. "And no one ever made you feel like I did, either."

"Not even close." Her desire to be near him screamed from every line of her willing body.

He shook his head at his own stupidity and her stubbornness. They could have had *this* for the last year. "Yet you broke it off with me."

"Because you offered a definitive ending date."

"And that wasn't something you wanted." She was really hung up on that concept.

He needed to remember that.

"No."

He didn't point out he was offering something very different this time. She knew it.

Just as he knew that ultimately, she would agree to marry him.

The draw between them was irresistible. He'd provided a way for them to meet, to connect, but one way or another, they would have come together again. It had been inevitable.

One day she might even admit that.

He forced himself to step back, to create physical space between them. He wanted her surrender, but if he accepted too early, they weren't going to make it the steps it would take to go from his office to his bedroom.

Romi seemed to understand that instinctively as well, as she looked around his personal space with dazed eyes that slowly cleared.

She moved to the photos gracing one of the built-in bookshelves. "Oh, my gosh…this is you as a little boy. With your mom."

She reached out and touched the photo with the same delicacy her hands showed on his body.

Pleasure shuddered through him. "I told you I was a child once."

"And an adorable one at that." He wasn't sure what the wistfulness in her voice was about.

"Mama thought so."

Romi threw him a smile over her shoulder before going back to the pictures. "This man, he's the one isn't he? The one that went away?"

He knew the photo she was talking about. It was of Natalya, Maxwell and the man he had called *Batya* for three years. They were on a harbor tour about a year after *Batya* had come into their lives.

Maxwell could remember *Batya* pointing out the landmarks and telling his eight-year-old self things the guide didn't mention. It had been a magical day.

"I'm surprised you have it out." Romi's voice was soft, her sympathy not grating like it would be from someone else.

"It is part of my history." A part he had never allowed himself to forget. Not the good times, not the way he'd felt when *Batya* simply wasn't there any longer, nor the years that followed.

"And putting it away wouldn't change that."

"No. Besides, it was a good day."

"Have you ever spoken to him since he left?"

"He died. No one told us. Why would they? Mama saw the obituary and told me. He was barely fifty."

"Oh, Max." That look on her face. It should have been like sandpaper on a raw wound, but he felt something warm unfurl inside him instead.

She crossed to him and walked right into his embrace, no sexual overtones to her actions, just a pure compassion that could only come from a pure heart like hers.

Romi's hands locked behind his neck, her head tilted back. "Do you know how old I was when Maddie and I decided to be sisters?"

He shook his head, strangely reluctant to speak, shocked at the fact he wasn't kissing her despite their positions. No other woman could derail his libidinous nature to something softer.

She said he was dangerous to her, but really, the opposite was just as true. He might never have the honesty to admit it, but he wasn't a fool to hide from reality, either.

"Five," she said, answering her own question.

"That is a long time ago." His voice came out oddly scratchy.

"Yes." Guileless blue eyes met his. "Almost twenty years."

He nodded.

"When I care about someone, I stay in his or her life. I don't give up because it's uncomfortable, or inconvenient." Those same blue eyes compelled him to believe in something other than the past.

He found himself wanting to and that only made him

more wary. "She did not have another family she had to give you up to keep."

"No, but if you think living with my dad the past few years has been a picnic, you're wrong. Or even being best friends with Madcap Madison. That girl scares the crap out of me sometimes, but I will never just walk out of her life."

Maxwell opened his mouth to tell her that their relationship wasn't the same, but closed it again without speaking.

One year ago, Romi had turned down his offer of a liaison with a time limit, but not once in the past twelve months had she tried to avoid him. If she saw him at an event, she spoke to him. She answered the phone when he called, though she'd made it clear it wasn't easy on her when he did call.

The queen of avoidance didn't avoid people.

It was an important realization to make.

"You are very special," he told her.

Her smile was luminescent. "I'm just me, but I've got to tell you, Max, I'm learning more about you in an afternoon than I have in all the time I've known you."

"You're going to marry me. You should know me."

"Arrogant much?" she mocked.

"We've already discussed this."

She sighed, but didn't look annoyed. Just accepting. "Make love to me, Max. I want to know what I'll learn about you then."

He didn't think there was much more for her to learn, but he wasn't about to turn her down.

He'd only said *no* in the car because in no dimension of time was one night going to be enough between the two of them.

Romi gasped out a laugh as Maxwell lifted her into his arms to carry her through to the bedroom.

"What are you doing?" she demanded breathlessly.

"My patience is at an end and we are going to do this right."

"I'm not your bride." Not yet.

"I am making you mine tonight. If that is not marriage, what is?"

She almost snarked that she thought it was a business contract where he was concerned, but the expression in his dark gray eyes stopped her.

There was no humor there, no uncertainty, just burning possession and desire. She'd known he was like this. Had found it almost impossible to resist and just as difficult to forget.

"We're making you mine, too, right?"

"Oh, yes, *milaya*, this is a two-sided promise we are making with our bodies."

"You've had sex with lots of women."

"More than a couple," he admitted without shame.

"You didn't claim them."

"For the hours we spent together their bodies were mine to pleasure, but the connection lasted only as long as the sex." He carried her into the bedroom and the moment felt as profound as he claimed.

She reflexively tightened her arms around his neck. "You're staking a different kind of claim on me."

"I did so a year ago."

"Did you really?"

"Oh, yes."

She believed him. Had no space to deny it. If she were honest with herself, she'd acknowledge she'd felt the claim and had lived with the hope that time would dull it into extinction.

Only now could she admit that hadn't happened with anything like speed or success. And he was intent on renewing that claim, taking it to the natural conclusion.

A claim she was pretty sure she would never be able to

dismiss again. Even with her best techniques at ignoring realities she did not want to face.

"You said you dated." If the claim went both ways, that shouldn't have happened.

Should it?

"I didn't say those dates ended in sex."

Shock coursed through Romi. "You haven't been celibate a year."

"I haven't?"

"Don't tease me. Just tell me." She needed it spelled out in that voice of his she knew never lied to her.

"Yes, Ramona. A year ago, you claimed my body and it wants only you now. Does that make you happy?" He sure didn't seem thrilled by the knowledge.

But Romi? She was a lot happier about it than his blackmail marriage proposal. "You know I didn't want anyone else, either."

"So, now we give in to the irresistible force."

"I thought that was *you*," she teased.

"So did I, before you engendered a burning desire in me that would not be quenched."

The kiss that followed sent fire licking through her and touched to the depths of her soul as his mouth claimed hers with a marauder's enthusiasm. When it ended, she was lying on the center of his huge bed, her clothes rumpled by his insistence on connecting with skin.

Gray irises almost swallowed completely by black, he perused her form with blatant possession and undeniable passion. Shoes gone, trousers open at the waist, Max's shirt was unbuttoned to reveal the dark whorls of hair on his muscular chest.

Moving to sit up, he reached out and she found both her hands caught in his. She looked down at their laced fingers and then back up to his handsome face.

His expression was borderline stunned, something about

the moment beyond what he had clearly expected. That was okay. Romi wasn't feeling all that steady herself.

"This is my pledge to you," he said and her heart stopped.

A pledge was a vow, a promise from a man who didn't break his word. She wasn't ready for promises, but couldn't find the words to deny him the moment.

"For as long as we are together, there will be no other," he said, all promise, no hesitation. "Any children we have will call *me* papa and be secure in my presence in their lives until the day I die."

Tears burned at the back of her eyes. "You're not being fair."

Pledges like this could not be dismissed the next day like cobwebs on the wind. Not even when a lesser man made them, much less a man of Maxwell Black's character.

"For as long as you belong to me, I will belong to you," he continued as if she had not spoken. "Your well-being will be my priority, your pleasure my desire, your happiness my goal."

"Even while you're blackmailing me with my dad's health?" she asked helplessly.

Gray eyes burned with certainty. "Even then."

"Stop making me promises." *Please stop*, her heart cried. "Just…just make love to me."

"You can deny it, but the truth will not change. This…" He pulled one hand away to point between the two of them. "This is bigger than sex, this is bigger than a single night's mind-blowing passion."

"That almost sounds like you are admitting to having a heart."

"Nyet," he denied in uncompromising Russian. "But a soul? Yes, that I have. Somehow, Ramona Grayson, you have found the way to touch it."

Even if he thought that would end one day, that their marriage wasn't about being soul mates, that admission right there was a better reason to take a chance on this man than all the blackmail in the world.

The kiss that followed was another promise in itself. A vow between the two of them that could not be pretended or ignored away. No matter what tomorrow brought, this moment would change Romi fundamentally and not just because she was taking her first lover.

The kiss didn't just hint, but it *vowed* the kind of passion a person could go her entire life without experiencing.

He lifted his lips from hers, but kept his body close, his gaze intent and determined in the way she remembered. "Tell me."

She remembered that demand, too, but somehow she knew that right now it meant more than playing a sensual game.

Max had made his promises. Now he would have hers.

"Yours."

"Only mine."

"Only yours."

He didn't ask for more, didn't demand she guarantee to be a good or even present mother. It was all covered in that single declaration, minimal words laden with complicated and far-reaching commitments. And she could not make herself regret that truth.

Whatever tomorrow might bring.

They undressed one another like old lovers, though they'd never been fully naked together before. When they'd dated, their times of intimacy had been explosive and unplanned.

Which wasn't to say they hadn't been intense, amazing and ultimately absolutely unforgettable.

But they'd never come to his penthouse to make love. She'd known where he lived, had even been in his building to wait for him, but never in his home, and definitely not his bedroom.

It felt so natural, though, to push his shirt off his shoulders, to tug his dangling belt from the loops on his trousers, that she did it all without any real thought.

And when he drew her tunic mini off, she didn't try to cover her small breasts, which were encased in a white silk bra designed to lift them into prominence. Not because she'd worn it for the very purpose of enticing him, either, but because she felt no need to hide. No desire for false barriers between them.

Max's eyes flared with heat as he traced the path of the lace covering the upper swells with one masculine finger. "Very pretty. I don't remember your lingerie being this sexy."

"I knew what I wanted." She didn't even blush when she said it.

She'd had plans for this afternoon and that shouldn't come as a shock to the unparalleled tsar of plan making.

The air around them vibrated with sensual hunger as her words seemed to impact him in a wholly favorable way.

"I like it." He leaned down and placed a kiss on the tip of her nipple, the heat from his breath drawing it into a tight bead. "Very much."

"Thank you."

"But it too must come off." Suiting action to words, he unclasped her bra and drew the silk away from her body.

She shivered in reaction to the feel of air on her nipples and his fingertips on her skin.

"You are so responsive," he said with masculine satisfaction.

"To you."

"As it should be." He cupped her breasts, his big hands holding her gently but with unmistakable possession. "Here? Have others touched you like this?"

"What?" Why was he asking her that?

"You said I am not like other men. I asked you how you knew," he reminded her, like he could read her confusion on her face.

Probably, he could.

"I…not like this. Under my shirt. Not my bra." The words shivered out of her as he squeezed carefully, kneading her breasts and pulling more pleasure from her.

"I am different from other men, but *milaya*, I think your response to me is unique as well, yes?"

"Oh, yes," she breathed softly.

"I will erase the touch of any other man, no matter how intimate."

How did she tell him he didn't need to erase what had never been there? She wasn't a total novice, or at least had always told herself the kissing and clothed petting meant she wasn't one. But Romi had been fooling herself.

This was sexual foreplay that would change her.

The other touches had left no lasting impact.

She tried to tell him that, but the words came out disjointed as Max removed her leggings and panties in one deft movement before tossing them aside.

"Shh…I understand. You are mine. I am yours. It is good." He pressed his finger to her lips, but then followed it almost immediately with his lips.

The kiss wasn't long, but it was thorough and she was squirming with passion's renewal when he pulled back.

His smile was full primeval predator. "It goes both ways, never doubt it."

"You're erasing the memory of other women in your bed?"

"No."

She couldn't stifle the sound of hurt.

He pressed her naked body to his still partially clothed one. "You cannot erase what has never been."

The words were an eerie match to her own thoughts only seconds before and an atavistic shiver trembled through her, but he could not mean them. "You've been with lots of other women."

"Never in this bed. Never with the knowledge that they owned my future."

No matter how fleeting that ownership might be, Romi couldn't help appreciating the sentiment. "Good."

He nodded, but he wasn't done. "Never has a woman responded to me like you do. Never has my own control been so tested, in the bedroom or out of it."

He'd said things like that before, but she'd never taken it to mean much. Now she realized it really was important to him. It helped explain why he'd overcome his own relationship boundaries to offer marriage, even marriage with a time-relative, easy-out clause.

"I like testing your control."

His laughter was deep and sexy. "No doubt."

Max stepped off the bed to remove the rest of his clothes and she didn't insist she get to do it. One thing she'd learned a year ago was she got extremely excited by his take-charge attitude in the bedroom. It had bothered her a year ago and maybe that was part of the reason she *hadn't* been willing to compromise her own ideas about relationships even though she'd wanted to so badly.

He didn't return to the bed immediately once he'd stripped, but stood in proud nudity and allowed her to look her fill. Like he knew she was craving just the sight of him.

Considering how well he'd known her every desire a year ago, she guessed he probably did.

Women were supposed to be less visual than men. Romi wasn't sure who had decided that. All she knew was that the sight of Max was as tantalizing as a touch for her.

She loved his height, the definition of his muscles, the contrast of his fair Russian skin to his dark hair, the way he held himself with such confidence. And she adored the way his chest was covered in short, dark, silky curls. The hair narrowed to a *V* and then followed a tapered trail that led to the patch surrounding his engorged sex. Flushed with blood, it stood out from his body in truly impressive proportions.

"You are devouring me with your eyes, *milaya*."

Was she? "You're a beautiful man." No other word fit as perfectly the work of art that Maxwell Black was naked.

From the dark hair that tempted her fingers to run through it, to the features she saw in her dreams and fantasies both, to a body covered in muscle from shoulders, to eight-pack rippling down his stomach, to thighs and calves that would make a professional athlete proud, he was complete and utter masculine perfection.

Perfection who claimed she touched something in his soul.

How soon before the feelings inside her coalesced into love so indomitable it would never end?

She didn't know, but she refused to allow her fear of that kind of inescapable emotion stop her from reveling in every incredible sensation this moment had to offer.

"You lay there like a goddess and call me beautiful?" There was that dark, sexy laugh again.

"Hardly a goddess."

"You inflame my senses." There was not an ounce of sarcasm or cheesy innuendo in his tone.

Romi rolled to her side facing him and propped her head on her hand. "That's pretty poetic for a business tycoon."

She bent her knee and let it rest on the bed, her upper thigh crossing her lower one, giving her best "sexy goddess" imitation, which was very close to one of her favorite yoga poses.

His gray eyes sparked with approval. "I thought we agreed I am a Corporate Tsar."

"And tsars are poetic in bed?" she wondered aloud.

"This one is, apparently."

Privately, she agreed, pretty sure that under all those tycoon smarts and ruthlessness, lived the soul of a poet.

She brushed her hand up her own thigh and over her hip. "Are you coming back to bed?"

"Are you so sure you want to poke the bear?" he asked in a very bearlike rumble.

"If it gets you closer to me? Oh, yes." She liked looking, but now she wanted to touch.

To be touched.

"You know what they say…"

"Be careful what you wish for," she said.

In a smooth movement worthy of a jungle cat—no lumbering bear—Max joined her on the bed. "You just might get it."

He pressed against her shoulder so she fell back, adjusted her legs so there was room for him between them and blanketed her with his body, every maneuver confident and determined.

They both stilled so only their breathing caused the slightest movement. He felt so right over her, his body big and strong, fitting perfectly against hers.

Max's head dipped until their foreheads touched, their breaths mingling in excited pants. "I want to consume you."

"Yes, please." This is what she *wanted*, had wanted for a lot longer than she'd admitted to herself.

His kiss was beyond consuming; it was voracious and domineering and filled with unbearable need. Not only was she helpless to deny that need, but Romi could also not help matching it. Desire whooshed through in a wildfire that nothing but full and total consummation and satisfaction would have any hope of putting out.

Her hands roamed restlessly over him, mapping him with touch everywhere she could reach, the heat of his body translating back to hers. Every caress only fed her need to touch him more so that her hunger increased into a conflagration of unsatisfied longing.

He held her head in place as their mouths continued to meet in a passion so strong, it obliterated everything else.

The world around them ceased to exist as lips and tongues tangoed to a sensual tune old as time and fresh as an infant's first smile.

At some point, he took hold of her hands and drew them upward until they rested over her head. Her initial inclination to fight the restriction drowned under the onslaught of desire that washed through her in response to him taking control.

Holding her wrists together with one hand, Max began to touch her in ways she remembered and others she did not.

There was no limit to the intimacy of his caresses, no spot on her body too private, and so many unexpected erogenous zones that elicited astonishing increases in her ardor. He explored her body, provoking reaction with every brush of his fingertips, bringing every single nerve ending online until her body was screaming with the demand for more.

"Maxwell," she gasped, not sure exactly what she was asking for, but knowing she needed *more.*

He lifted away from her and that was *not* what she wanted. She tried to reach for him, but he still had her wrists pinned.

She made a sound of frustration she'd never heard from herself before. "What are you doing?" Oh, gosh…she was *whining.*

Romi did not whine. Never had.

He didn't seem annoyed, though. His expression was too intent for any other emotion than desire. "I want to give you pleasure beyond your wildest imagining."

"I'm pretty sure we're already there."

"I want more. Don't you, *dorogaya*?"

"You know I do." He was the one who had moved away.

"Then you must trust me."

She opened her mouth and found herself bewilderingly bereft of answer. He didn't seem to notice as he released her hands and stepped back from the bed.

He turned away and opened a drawer in a dark wood

cabinet. When he turned back, he had a pile of cerulean blue silk in his hand.

"What is that for?" she asked in a voice roughened by passion.

He shook out the fabric and she saw that it was two long scarves, the silk so fine it rippled on the air with the slightest movement.

CHAPTER EIGHT

"I BOUGHT THESE months ago," Max replied in a musing tone. "I should have known then."

"Known what?" Romi asked.

"That you were not going to get out of my head."

"Okay." Assimilating the fact that the silk was the exact shade of her eyes when she was happy, Romi chewed on her bottom lip. "Um, what are they for?"

"Your pleasure."

"You want to tie me up." She shouldn't have been startled.

He had given her tremendous pleasure before by accepting control and using it to her benefit. She *wasn't* shocked. Not really.

She also wasn't sure *how* she felt about the scarves.

He must have read the ambivalence in her face because he said persuasively, "Just your hands."

"Not this time." She wasn't sure why, but she knew those scarves represented something between them that wasn't there yet.

He reeled back, as if her words *had* shocked him, maybe even *hurt* him. "You enjoyed me being in control very much a year ago."

"Yes." There was no denying it.

Romi wouldn't even try to deny that she got a special sexual thrill out of the attention he gave her, the way she became his entire focus when that happened. But she wasn't ready for the scarves, either.

She *really* wasn't sure why. One time, when they'd been dating, he'd used his tie to bind her hands behind her back while he touched her. She'd loved it.

He'd brought her to a mind-shattering climax, quickly followed by another.

And still, she wasn't going for the scarves right now.

He sat beside her, running the silk over her body, bringing forth shivers of sensation she made no attempt to stifle. "A year ago, you would not have hesitated."

"I know."

"So?" he prompted, clearly expecting her to change her mind.

It was that confidence that coalesced at least a partial understanding of her hesitancy for that type of game right now.

"Maybe I trusted you more before you offered my father's sobriety only to turn around and threaten it, or before you threatened to take advantage of my best friend's desire to protect me from her dad." Romi wasn't accusing, or trying to pick a fight, just stating the facts.

And maybe the fact he was trying to blackmail her into his version of marriage bothered her more than she'd realized. She *didn't* accept that he was a monster, but that didn't mean he couldn't hurt her with his single-minded view of the world and insistence of having his own way.

In fact, she was pretty sure he *could*.

The silk pooled on her stomach in a pile of fabric so light she barely felt it.

Frowning, he ran his hands down her body in a move that seemed wholly unconscious, hurt he probably didn't even realize was there shadowing his gray gaze. "The one has nothing to do with the other."

That hurt gave her hope, but didn't sway her certainty that she had hold firm on this. "You are too intelligent and understanding of human nature to believe that."

"*Dorogaya*, your pleasure is my top priority."

"You've never used that word before," she said because she'd rather focus on that than his claim. A claim she believed, but was not the point. "What does it mean?"

"Sweetheart."

"So, more intimate than *milaya*?" She hoped she'd pronounced that right.

"Yes. Why? Does it matter?"

"You know it does."

His use of this new Russian endearment was no coincidence, but was it by design or necessity to satisfy the poet in his soul?

He nodded, acknowledging that it did matter. "You do not wish me to use the scarves?"

"No."

"I have never used them with another woman."

She liked hearing that more than she would ever admit. "That isn't why I don't want to use them right now."

"You do not trust me."

"I'm not sure."

"You are punishing me."

"I don't think so." But she wouldn't give an unequivocal denial because she wasn't sure if she wasn't. At least a little.

He studied her measuringly for several long seconds before scooping up the silk, his fingers brushing over her abdomen with a clearly deliberate movement. "We will leave the restraints in the drawer for now."

"Okay."

"You know you only ever have to say *no* if you want me to stop doing *anything*."

"I believe you." They'd never needed a safe word.

Romi had once asked him if he ever played that way and he'd told her sex was not a game to him.

Despite the undeniable sensual games he played, she believed that. He wouldn't want a safe word because to Maxwell Black, respecting the word *no* was as important as keeping his word.

"I will know you trust me when you pull them out." And there was that hurt again, but he seemed no more aware of it.

She nodded, her throat suddenly gone too dry to answer.

He took the blue silk away and part of her regretted it, but not enough to stop him.

If her refusal bothered him on a conscious level, it didn't show. His erection had not flagged, his expression as filled with primal desire as ever. He came back to her, but didn't blanket her with his body as he'd done before.

Instead, he leaned over her to adjust her hands above her head, one clasping the other wrist. "Okay?" he asked.

She jerked her head in affirmative. "Mmm-hmm."

"Keep them there." It wasn't a question.

She answered anyway. "All right."

With a gentle, but inexorable touch, he separated her thighs, opening her in unambiguous familiarity. She was *his*. "You are so very lovely."

"Thank you." Her voice was husky. So strange. So not like her usual perky tones.

He brushed his fingers through the curls at the apex of her thighs and she jolted. Who knew her *hair* could be sensitive, but did that feel *good*? It felt amazing.

He leaned down and breathed in deeply. "I want the fragrance of your desire."

"Um, okay," she practically whispered. She felt like maybe she should be embarrassed, but there was no room for that kind of reaction between them.

There was too much honest need.

"There is a school of sexual thought that claims there are four different areas of the foot that are particularly sexually stimulating. Did you know that?" he asked as he gently pressed into one that sent a sensual frisson straight up her inner thigh and into her core.

"No, oh...ohhh..." Her answer tailed off into a moan as he found another.

"I'm an eclectic learner," he said almost conversationally, but the forceful desire in his dark metallic-gray eyes removed any casual feel to the words.

"Ye-esss?"

"I studied the pressure points of the body with a master of Dim Mak who had made it his life's work to also discover the unexpected areas of the body that could give the most pleasure."

"Aren't pressure points about pain?" she asked uncertainly.

"Knowing them is as important for avoidance as knowing those touches that can bring the greatest pleasure. I will never take you over that edge between pleasure and pain, though sometimes the ecstasy is going to be so great, you will wonder how close you are."

"Oh." She stared at him in shock, which she knew reflected her own innocence. "You studied how to have sex?"

"Not just sex, *dorogaya*, but amazing, mind-melting sex."

"The kind that makes you feel like you've had an out-of-body experience." She could remember that from a year ago and they hadn't even had intercourse.

His smile was both pleased and predatory. "Yes."

"But you're a Corporate Tsar. When did you have time?"

"Everyone needs a hobby. Naturally, my teacher also trained me in traditional kung fu."

No wonder his body was so buff. "It was part of your exercise regimen then." Even so, it was a little mind-boggling that Max had made a study of sex.

"Yes."

"That's a lot of work for part-time lovers." Her words rose and fell several octaves as his touch grew more intimate, moving up to her inner thighs.

He shrugged, but she saw something in his eyes.

And she had her answer. Or at least part of it. Just as she was excited by him taking control, Max got something out of it, too. "Your pleasure comes from controlling that of your partner."

"Part of it, yes."

Of course it would. A man like him, whose whole life was focused on control. Sex would be no different.

"Maybe you were just practicing for me?" She liked that thought more than that he'd given *this* part of himself to others before her.

It was *hers*. She wasn't sure where that possessive thought came from, but she did nothing to squelch it. Evidence to the contrary, it wasn't as if he could read her mind anyway.

His sexy chuckle didn't sound even a little mocking. "I think perhaps you are right."

When he bypassed her most intimate flesh to move up her body, she wasn't surprised. He'd done this a year ago. Built her pleasure until she was aching for touches her innocent body had never known.

Even so, she couldn't hold back a sound of protest.

"Shh…" His caress moved up her waist, his expression so hot it burned. "We will get there, but you only have one first time."

He was going to tease her more than before?

She realized the words had come out in a plaintive wail when he shook his head decisively. "I am not teasing you, *dorogaya*. I am *pleasuring* you."

"Tom-ay-to, to-mah-to," she gasped out as his thumbs skimmed over her rigid nipples.

Her breasts were small, but they had discovered together that the peaks were extremely sensitive.

"No, no, no…it is not just a different way of saying the same thing," he assured her. "To tease is to make your partner wonder if you will ever give the bliss craved and you know I will."

"On your time frame," she gasped out.

"That is my way." He said it with that Russian pragmatism she found both appalling and ridiculously appealing by turns.

"Sometime, maybe you should let *me* use the blue scarves." Oh, gosh…every word required effort as his caresses grew more and more tantalizing.

He stopped, his entire being arrested by her comment. He looked down at her, an unreadable expression on his face. "I have never been open to another lover doing so."

"But me?" she asked, knowing his answer mattered very much, though not at all sure why.

After all, she didn't really want to use the scarves on him; she much preferred it the other way around.

"Yes." Their gazes locked, as intimate as any caress. "Sometime, yes."

Elation filled her, but she just *knew* if he saw it, he would mistake it for triumph. Which isn't how she felt at all, so she did her best to simply nod and say, "I think I might like that."

"We will see, won't we?"

Yes, they would. But not today. Today, they would make love his way and she would give him the gift of her innocence. She didn't care if that was an old-fashioned way to look at it, she suspected he saw it the same way.

He kissed her then, whether it was to stop the conversation, or simply because that was the next step in her very willing seduction, she didn't know. What she did know was that it short-circuited her brain, which was already overloaded with pleasure.

His mouth possessed hers with the power of any tsar laying claim to his territory. Thrillingly. Absolutely. And with unmistakable intent.

Max's caresses became more zealous, taking on a feverish edge and increasing the delight to her senses when she would have said the latter was impossible. But something deep inside her basked in the tangible proof of the knowledge he wanted to make her his own.

She wasn't sure when her hands moved from above her head so she could wrap her arms around him, doing a little claiming of her own. Instead of stopping, as he might have done a year ago, Max's touches turned even more passionate and less controlled.

Part of her reveled in that, but the rest of her just enjoyed the next level of sexual delight it inspired.

Romi's hands lost purchase on Max as he moved to follow the touch of his hands with that of his mouth. Masculine lips, talented tongue and careful teeth teased already sensitive flesh until she was whimpering with need.

And not in the least embarrassed by that fact.

He nuzzled into the apex of her thighs, making a fully masculine sound of satisfaction. Then he parted her with his fingers before flicking his tongue against her clitoris and she tried to come up off the bed.

Her cry echoed around them as he continued to kiss her in the most intimate way possible. His fingers slipped inside her, the only flesh besides her doctor's that had ever been *inside* Romi's body.

There was no impediment to his deep finger thrusting. There wouldn't be after years in gymnastics.

The only area she and Maddie had diverged. Maddie had played soccer and softball. Romi had competed in gymnastics until her height decreed she would be able to take those aspirations no further.

Along the way, her inner barrier had stretched and finally broken, she was sure.

All thoughts of the whys and wherefores exploded in a cataclysm of bliss that had her shaking and screaming.

He gentled her through the climax and took her beyond to another layer of pleasure on the cusp of orgasm. Again.

Only then did he move to settle between her thighs, his swollen member pressing against the entrance to her body. His expression was every bit as possessive as his position. "This is mine, *dorogaya*. Your innocence will never belong to another."

She wouldn't, either, in any way, she was sure of it. But there was no point in telling him. He was still laboring under the mistaken impression that if they married, it would be a temporary if years-long condition.

She knew better. Right then, she knew to the very depths of her soul *and* heart that this man would always be hers and vice versa. He might never let himself love her and that would inevitably bring pain with it.

But their souls were already entwined.

He didn't ask if she was ready. He didn't say anything at all. He just looked down at her with eyes that claimed, demanded and pleaded all at the same time.

The demand excited her in a way others might not understand, but the pleading she was sure he had no knowledge of. That decided her beyond a shadow of any possible doubt that the time had come to join their bodies.

"Please," she said to and for Max.

He nodded and began pushing inside, the wide girth of his shaft stretching her as she had never been stretched before. It felt so right, the link between their souls causing her body to accommodate his, his big frame surrounding her to make that connection even more intimate and perfect.

Romi didn't realize how long it had been since she felt truly safe until the moment when any sense of being alone and having to protect herself and those around her was gone completely.

Maxwell wasn't a tsar. He was her own personal Cossack. Bloodthirsty in his face to the world, but a wall between her and anything that might hurt her.

Even his own threats.

Where that certainty came from, she again did not know, but her inner conviction was absolute.

He made love to her with care, but also with a passion that grew increasingly unbridled until they strained together in an act millions of others engaged in every day, but still felt unique to them.

Special.

No one else would ever affect her as he did.

And no other woman would draw this lack of control, this unplanned, unmeasured movement and reaction from Maxwell Black.

Her pleasure built in proportion to the emotional intimacy she felt despite the lack of love words between them. She wasn't ready to acknowledge that feeling if it did reside in her heart. However, the invisible threads this intimate act was building between them went deeper than romance.

They were stronger than any words, even *I love you*. She would never live another day of her life without feeling a bond with this man.

Even if they didn't live in the same house and never again shared their bodies.

Was that because she was a virgin? She didn't know and didn't care.

It simply was.

Rapture built between them, their breathing growing more erratic, a sheen of sweat washing over their bodies, the physical heat between them growing by degrees. Her own heart was beating so fast and hard, she could feel it in her ears. She knew his tempo would mirror hers if she laid her hand against his heart, but holding onto his shoulders as they mated was taking all her coordination.

Suddenly that feeling, that ecstasy only he had brought forth, was right there, ready to burst inside her.

"Maxwell," she cried as she thrust up to meet him.

"Give it to me, *dorogaya*. Now." His voice was fractured and harsh with need.

She had no thought to deny him, bliss shattering through her, destroying the last defense she may have had between them.

And then his big body went rigid, his throat corded, his jaw clenched, before he gave a loud shout and came, too.

It was the most profound moment of her life. She had never felt this close to anyone. Not to her family, not to her SBC, not to anyone.

"Dorogaya." Max collapsed on top of her, whispering Russian into Romi's hair.

She welcomed the weight, not really caring how hard it was to breathe in that moment. She didn't know what he was saying, but she recognized the endearments he'd used with her and wallowed in the emotional warmth that poured through her with each utterance.

Sometime later, Max lifted away only enough to come down beside her, wrapping his body possessively around hers.

"That was amazing," she said, though it was probably pretty obvious to him that he'd melted her brain along with her nerve endings.

"It was." He sounded a little surprised by his own admission.

She didn't say anything, just snuggled in, feeling like she couldn't get close enough.

"We did not use a condom," he said, no regret in his tone, just stating a fact.

"No, we didn't."

"We will in future, but for your first time there should be no barriers between us."

And he said he had no romance in his soul. "I could still get pregnant," she pointed out, but with no heat.

"If you do, you do. We are getting married regardless. If you do not, we will wait some time for our first child."

"You think that's your decision to make alone?" she asked, not upset, because she *didn't* and he'd figure that out, but wondering.

"No. Do you disagree?"

"No."

"I thought not."

Hmmm…maybe he just *knew* some things, too.

"Which is not to be taken as an agreement from me on your highly irregular marriage proposal," she reminded him.

"Duly noted." He flipped her onto her back and looked down at her, his eyes dark with an unexpected renewed passion. "But for now, let's keep on testing our physical compatibility."

Oh, man, as if that was in any kind of question. She didn't say anything like that, though. Romi just returned kiss for kiss and this time around he seemed content for her to return caress for caress, too.

Later, she was grateful for his height and strength as they showered together. Her legs were as rubberized as if she'd run a full-length marathon.

Other muscles felt just as used, too.

She sure wasn't going to feel bad about missing her evening workout for the day.

He made dinner and it wasn't just soup out of a tin, either. He grilled chicken on the balcony to his penthouse, while rice finished in the cooker, and then sautéed asparagus in olive oil and garlic.

She smiled at him as they ate. "I'm impressed."

"That I can cook?"

"Yes. I'm pretty sure it's not your typical skill set for a Corporate Tsar."

He shrugged. "I don't like keeping staff on site. Besides, cooking relaxes me."

"I've heard that." She wasn't sure she saw the appeal.

"Don't you cook?"

"Nope. We always had a housekeeper." Mrs. K had come to work for them when Romi was in primary school, but there had never been a time when her father didn't employ someone in the position.

Romi was definitely no one's idea of a domestic goddess.

"We didn't."

She sidled up to him, enjoying the way his arm came out to automatically pull her into his side. "You don't sound like that bothers you."

"It doesn't, but since I wasn't raised with them, I'm more apt to find household help intrusive than not."

"You don't do your own cleaning." No way.

His smile was sardonic. "No."

"I didn't think so."

"Is it going to bother you?" Max asked her.

"What?"

"Not having live-in domestic help?"

"Is it going to bother you to do the cooking when we haven't arranged for a meal?" She didn't mind cleaning, or making her own bed, though admittedly she didn't very often, but that sort of thing was in her skill set.

Cooking wasn't.

"No."

"Then, no."

Later, Romi savored a bite of asparagus perfectly prepared. "I might have to take a cooking class someday. This is really delicious." Maybe Maddie would take the class with her.

"I am glad you like it." He ate his own food with little attention, his focus entirely on her. "I don't expect you to learn to cook. My housekeeper comes in daily and prepares most evening meals ahead of time."

"Good to know. *If* I decide to marry you."

He didn't get angry. In fact, humor played at the corners of his mouth. "Marriage will bring sufficient changes to your life without cooking."

"You don't say." She flicked him a flirtatious glance.

"Besides having a hell of a lot of sex, smart aleck."

"Did I say anything about sex?" Unaccountably, heat washed through her cheeks. She would have thought herself incapable of embarrassment about these things after their very long afternoon of lovemaking.

"You have a charming blush."

"Thanks?"

"You're not sure you appreciate my observation?"

"Not really, no. I think someone with more tact would have simply ignored my pink cheeks."

"I am not known for my tact."

"No, I don't imagine you are." She sipped at the crisp white wine he'd served with dinner. "So, you said *other* changes."

"You will have a security detail assigned to you."

"I'm sure that's not necessary."

He smiled, though there was very little humor in it. "I'm sure that it is."

"I can't attend, much less speak at a rally for lower CO_2 emissions with a bunch of security guys following me around."

"You can dress them in T-shirts with conservation slogans, but your team will be with you at all times you are away from home." He made it sound like that was going to start immediately.

She frowned. "You don't always have a detail."

"I do."

"What about last night? There was no gun-toting gorilla in the car with us."

"No, but there was a two-man team of highly trained professional personal security agents in the car behind us. They parked at the end of the driveway."

"Oh. Were they in the ballroom?"

"No. Viktor had security covered for the reception. My detail got a couple of hours to do what they wanted. They didn't leave the hotel, though."

"Oh." So, that argument had gone nowhere. "Does your mom have security?"

"Mama has a bodyguard."

"Natalya wouldn't agree to a full detail, would she?"

Max's frown said it all.

That was more promising. "Couldn't I just have a body-guard, too?"

"I prefer a two-man detail when you are away from home."

Or not. "Isn't that a ridiculous expenditure?"

"Nothing like paying out a ten-million-dollar ransom."

"Like you'd pay that to get me back." Seriously.

Max just looked at her.

No. He couldn't mean it. He had to be talking out of his hat. "Why would you?" Did they even have kidnapping insurance that went that high?

"You're talking like this is a done deal." His look wasn't quite a smile, but it was definitely triumphant.

Still, she recognized Max's conversational tactic. She'd used it herself. "I know what you are doing."

Max didn't want to answer her and so pushed the conversation in a direction he knew she didn't want to go.

"You'll be spending the night." He looked at her clothes, or lack thereof significantly.

She'd donned one of his dress shirts after dinner. Burgundy silk, it felt good against her skin and well, she *liked* the fact that it was Max's.

Romi had been wearing it since before Max started cooking, the fact he brought it up now indicated he *really* didn't want to talk about the fact he would pay such a ridiculously high sum to get her back.

Nevertheless, she stored that bit of information away, along with how matter-of-fact he'd been about it. He hadn't hesitated for a moment and that meant something, didn't it?

CHAPTER NINE

AFTER DINNER, ROMI texted Jeremy Archer and asked if she could schedule a phone call with him the next day.

He must have forwarded the text to his administrative assistant because that's who sent a time for the phone call to Romi.

Romi couldn't help comparing the response to how her dad would have reacted to a text from Maddie. First, Maddie *wouldn't* have had to schedule the phone call, not even back in the day when he was working at Grayson Enterprises full-time.

Second, if Romi's dad had been that busy, *he* would have texted to say so and schedule the time.

Even with the drinking, she much preferred Harry Grayson as a parent over Jeremy Archer.

Warm hands slid around to settle on her stomach and Max's hard body pressed against her back. "What are you thinking?"

She told him.

"You really mean that, don't you?" Max asked, sounding surprised.

She turned in his arms. "Parenting is about more than providing money for the best schools and someone to cook nutritious meals."

"I agree."

"Good."

"My mother set a very good example."

"Well, you may not believe it, but my dad did, too."

"I would not discount your childhood memories because your father has slid so deeply into the bottle in recent years."

"Thank you." She smiled. "So, we agree…children deserve their parents to be fully engaged in parenting."

"Yes."

"My dad did a great job raising me without my mom."

"And my mother did a stellar job without my sperm donor," he replied drily.

"But if we make babies together, they get both of us."

"Absolutely."

"Even if we don't stay together." She would say it so he didn't have to.

His muscles contracted around her, pulling her close against him. "Especially then."

He didn't seem to notice how tight he was holding her. An unconscious reaction to her words? Maybe.

Maybe Max didn't like thinking about ending the marriage she hadn't agreed to yet any more than she did.

She looked up at him through her lashes and leered playfully. "Wanna do some more compatibility testing?"

His eyes going molten, Max didn't even crack a smile. His answer was to simply bend down and lift her into his arms, heading toward the bedroom without delay. She hooked one arm around his broad shoulders and leaned forward to place soft little kisses against the side of his neck.

She inhaled deeply of his masculine scent. He'd shaved again before dinner and the faint traces of his aftershave added a woodsy fragrance.

Nuzzling into the scent, she flicked her tongue out to taste his skin. Salty and clean, it was all Max. The one man she wanted above all others.

Now, look who was being naff. But really? This man was it for her and she knew it.

The changing light indicated they'd come into the bedroom. Romi squirmed out of his arms before they could land on the bed together.

"What?" he demanded.

She pointed to the oversized brown leather armchair with matching ottoman in the corner. "Sit down over there."

He questioned her with his eyes, but he didn't argue. The chair was easily large enough to hold them both and yet he didn't look dwarfed in it at all.

His presence was so real, so overwhelming.

Corporate Tsar? Definitely. Maxwell Black would dominate the most ornate throne, not the other way around.

And she liked that with shameless enthusiasm.

She started to nudge the ottoman out of the way with her knee and suddenly it was sliding to the side, Max's foot shoving against it.

"Thank you," she told him.

He merely shrugged.

She tugged at the hem of his undershirt. "Here, let's take this off."

He'd put on a pair of sleep pants and black-ribbed man's tank top after their shower.

She loved the way the shirt clung to his muscles and exposed the hair she enjoyed so much, but she wanted him naked and this was the first, very necessary, step.

Max peeled it off and tossed the undershirt to the side. He gripped the waistband of his flannel sweats. "These, too, hmm?"

She nodded, happy he was on board with her plan. He might even know what her endgame was.

When he was naked, sitting on the chair, she dropped to her knees in front of him. Nostrils flaring, his jaw locked, bringing to mind that Cossack she'd likened him to earlier.

"You like me in this position," she tried teasing, but her own voice was husky with desire and anticipation.

Molten pewter locked onto her with laser intensity. "I like you any way I can get you."

"I believe you." And didn't that just make her want to do this more? Pressing against his knees, she asked, "Widen your legs for me?"

"You want to be in charge this time?" he asked, not sounding bothered by the fact. And not merely curious, either. More like intrigued.

"I want to experiment." Did that sound bad? "You're not just an experiment for me," she hastened to add.

"I know that." He let his thighs fall open, giving her an unhindered view of his rapidly growing erection and heavy balls below it. "I am at your disposal."

"So polite." Any mockery she'd meant to infuse her tone with was lost in her delight at his clear willingness to let her explore.

"For you."

"It's always just for me, isn't it?"

"Oh, yes." No doubt in his tone or expression.

She was special to him and despite his jaundiced view of relationships, he didn't hesitate to let her know it.

How was she going to keep any part of her heart from fixating on this man?

Unable to hold back any longer, Romi reached out and ran her finger down the hardening shaft and over the wrinkled skin lightly dusted with hair below. "It's so soft."

"This is what you call soft?" he asked teasingly, running his own hand over his engorged member. "It feels pretty hard to me."

Her breath caught at the sight. "I didn't mean that."

"No?" He let his hand fall away and laid both hands to rest on the arms of the chair, opening his body in an even more blatant invitation to her touch.

She shook her head, unable to form a verbal answer.

He was so perfect. So delicious. And so incredibly tempting. A temptation she had no impetus to hold back from giving in to.

Romi reached out to touch him again, this time like he

had. She curled her fingers around his steel-hard shaft. She loved the way he filled her hand, how his silky smooth skin felt so hot against the palm of her hand and pads of her fingers.

Running her hand up and down the intimate column of flesh, she elicited a low groan from him.

"I like touching you."

His grin was feral, triumphant, not amused. "I know, *dorogaya*."

She really loved the way he'd shifted to the more intimate endearment when they were making love.

And this was making love every bit as much as when he was buried inside her body. For her anyway.

She didn't know how he saw it, but she felt that same soul-deep connection.

Romi continued to run her hand up and down his erection until he was moaning steadily, tilting his hips up in silent supplication. She totally understood in that moment how exciting he could find giving pleasure to his lovers.

To her.

Seeing him react to *her* touch impacted her own desire like a matchstick to a bucket of gasoline.

Drunk on the power in a way wine never impacted her, she leaned forward and kissed the tip of his erection. Pearly liquid had formed and smeared on her lips. She flicked her tongue out to taste it. He groaned and swore in Russian.

"I like how you taste." She licked the remaining pearly liquid from her lips.

"I'm glad."

She dipped her head and did it again, this time tasting directly from the source. Salty. Sweet. *Maxwell*. A moment of intimacy she never wanted to know with another man.

Which said a lot about the *choice* she insisted she hadn't yet made.

Ignoring that thought, she took the head into her mouth, swirling her tongue around the circumference.

The sound that came out of Max was pure, visceral, primitive *need*. So, she kept doing just that, laving his bulbous tip with her tongue, bringing forth more sounds of passion and masculine pleasure.

"Move your hand on the shaft and suck." It was both masculine demand and plea.

Never had Romi heard instructions given in a tone of such raw desire.

No thought of denial entered her head. She gave him exactly what he asked for and discovered she enjoyed doing it. Very much.

No surprise there. She loved everything about touching this man.

Suddenly his hands were in her hair, tugging at her head. "Stop, Romi…please, *dorogaya*. You must stop."

She pulled back with reluctance and looked up at him. He shook his head, like he couldn't quite believe what was happening. "I'm too close to coming."

"Uh-huh." That was the point, wasn't it?

"You aren't ready for that. You may never want to taste me to that extent."

"Oh." She'd liked it so far, but she'd heard that a man's ejaculate was bitter.

Maybe it was a stronger flavor when he came?

She stopped her musing when he took both lapels of the silk dress shirt she wore in his hands and very deliberately, very slowly, pulled them apart so buttons and fabric gave.

Unbearably turned on, she did not move as he reached out to cup her small breasts, abrading her nipples with his thumbs. "You were made just for me."

That wasn't something she would ever deny. She wasn't the one who thought it was inevitable they would one day separate.

He sure wasn't thinking of separating right now.

He was thinking about her, his pewter gaze filled with desire *for* her, like she was all he could see.

With impressive strength that turned her on even more, he lifted her into his lap. Romi's knees fell to the sides of his thighs, his hands on her bottom holding her exactly where he wanted. Her own hands landed against his chest and she perched there, her body exposed for him.

He tugged her close to rub her soft, wet intimate flesh against his imposing hardness. Her clitoris met that hard masculine column of flesh, and pleasure jolted through her. He rocked his pelvis, stimulating the bundle of nerve endings until her breath was sobbing in and out in a vain effort to keep up with the speed of her heart.

She could climax like this, too easily. But that wasn't what she wanted.

Romi shifted with intent…Max lifted and tilted her…and then she was sliding down over him, her body once again stretching to accommodate his size. Encasing him in her most tender flesh, Romi held Max inside her, their physical connection complete.

The only sound between them their harsh breathing, hard fingers guided her hips into movement. "Come on, *dorogaya*. Move for me."

She obeyed because she couldn't do anything else, lifting and lowering her hips with jerky enthusiasm. Romi let him lead her into a rhythm that pleasured them both, bringing little bursts of ecstasy with every downward thrust of her hips and long moaning pleasure with every rise upward.

He praised her efforts until they climaxed again almost simultaneously, his rigidity and loss of control sending her over the edge into pure, unadulterated ecstasy. They froze there together in a tableau of rapture, her body slick with sweat, his pupils blown from sensation.

She didn't know how long they were like that, but eventually, Romi let herself fall forward and he caught her. Like she knew he would.

Max cradled her close against his body, his breathing still as harsh as her own. "We forgot the condom."

"Again," she panted.

"The first time we did not forget."

She didn't quibble. *She* had forgotten. He'd been looking to give her what she needed the first time they made love.

"Hopefully, it will be okay. It's the wrong time in my cycle." Her period had just ended a couple of days ago. She shouldn't be ovulating yet. She remembered that much from health class.

"We will be more careful."

She nodded against his chest. "Maybe we should keep condoms around the bedroom."

"Around the penthouse, more like."

She grinned where he could not see her, inordinately proud of herself. He thought they would lose control in just any room at any time. From a man of his controlling temperament, that was the ultimate compliment.

"You're pleased with yourself, aren't you?" he asked, a smile in his own voice.

"Well, your vaunted control hasn't been so much in evidence," she said modestly.

He laughed and it was only as she heard the rich sound and felt it rumble in his chest did she realize how wrongly he could have taken her words, or simply how offended he could have gotten. Because control really was a thing for this man.

"You put my control to the test. That is true."

"Does that make us *very* compatible or not very?" she asked, tongue in cheek, certain of the answer, not even a little bit worried.

"As if you did not know." He tilted her head up so their gazes met. "You're a handful, you know that?"

"I'm aware."

"Your father spoiled you."

"Sweet, not rotten. That's what Dad always said. He spoiled me sweet, not rotten."

Max's warm smile said he might just agree with the older Grayson.

Harry Grayson called at nine and cried when he spoke to Romi, but he made a promise, too. He promised to dry out and to try to make the program work.

"I know it's hard for you," she offered.

He made a sound of disagreement that surprised her until the words that followed. "Not as hard as losing my daughter to my weakness would be."

"I'm not going anywhere."

"At some point watching me destroy myself would hurt too much to stay."

His words shocked her. "No."

"Yes." He sighed, clearly trying to get ahold of himself. "Listen, kitten. All I've ever wanted for you was happiness."

"I know."

"You aren't going to be happy if I kill myself slowly with bourbon, no matter how good the year."

"Um, yeah…I could really care less how high-quality your liquor cabinet is."

"I know. You care about me." There was something in her dad's tone—an echo of the man who had raised her before his drinking had become such a consuming pastime.

"I love you, Daddy."

"I love you, too, kitten." Enough to try to get and stay sober.

He didn't have to say the words aloud. She heard them anyway and they gave her hope for the future with her dad she hadn't had in a long time.

They rang off and Max took her to bed, where he cuddled her for a long time before making love to her with such passion she forgot her own name right along with the phone call from her dad.

* * *

Max and Romi made love again the next morning before sharing breakfast and him insisting on driving Romi home before going into BIT.

He got out and came around to open her door with the kind of courtesy that usually either annoyed her or came off as fake. With Max it felt natural and she didn't mind it. Appreciated the gesture even.

He stopped at her door like he had the other night. "I will not come in." He smiled more naturally than she'd ever seen him, a tinge of mischief lighting the gorgeous dark gray of his eyes. "My schedule is too full this morning for a late start."

She shamelessly fluttered her lashes at him with a confidence born of their new intimacy. "Are you saying you can't resist me?"

"If I could resist you, I would not have spent a year pining."

Talk about exaggeration. If anyone had been pining, it had been her. Her best efforts to forget him notwithstanding. "Oh, be real, Max. Men like you don't pine."

"Call it what you like, but don't call it resisting you."

She nodded, touched in a way she was sure he had not intended. But that admission wasn't just about sex, no matter how he fooled himself.

Romi should know. She had spent her life avoiding things she didn't want to face. She recognized the signs.

But then maybe he wasn't trying to fool himself. He'd as good as said it was more than sex the day before. Not love. Oh, no. Not love for Maxwell Black, but it was definitely more than sex.

"I will pick you up for a late dinner," he said as he turned to go.

"We agreed. I need tonight to think." Not that she hadn't pretty much made up her mind, but he didn't need to know that.

He turned to face her at the bottom step. "You can think after dinner."

"That's not what we agreed."

"We didn't say no contact while you did your thinking."

"It was implied."

"No."

She opened her mouth to argue, but the words wouldn't come. To claim she didn't want to see him would be a lie. "Fine. But I'm not waiting until nine to eat. I'll expect you at seven."

His lips flatlined, but he nodded.

"Okay, see you then." She wasn't sure what to do with herself.

She should just turn around and go back inside, but she didn't want to. How pathetic would it be to stand there and watch him drive away?

Pretty pathetic, she figured, but that was what she was going to do anyway.

He'd have to get used to her foibles if he wanted to marry her, even if he planned to divorce her down the line.

Max's eyes narrowed, his jaw going hard, and then he was striding back up the steps. He didn't stop when he reached her, but took her into his arms and gave her a very thorough, very possessive kiss. "Seven o'clock. Pack an overnight bag."

"That's not the deal." But she was talking to his back and he didn't acknowledge the words before climbing back into the Maserati and driving away.

The phone call with Jeremy Archer was more than a little stilted. Romi was still angry with the corporate shark that treated his daughter like a bargaining chip on his game board.

"Where did you hear that?" he demanded after she'd asked if Maddie had made the threat to give her shares over to Harry Grayson.

"Does it matter?"

"My daughter didn't tell you. She wouldn't."

"If you know her that well, why didn't you know her well enough to handle this whole thing differently?"

"I don't need parenting advice from a child."

"You need it from someone," she told him with tactless honesty and not even a smidgen of guilt.

"She made the threat," he confirmed. "Why? Are you planning to capitalize on it?" he sneered. "It won't happen. That drunk isn't getting his hands on my company."

It was only twenty-five percent, but Romi didn't quibble particulars. She was too furious. "My dad is not a drunk!"

Jeremy's bark of laughter was harsh, clearly unconvinced.

It infuriated her. Her dad was an alcoholic, but he wasn't a waste of space, like this heartless man implied. "You were friends once."

"We still are," Jeremy said, sounding surprised she'd say that.

"You know the old saying, with *friends* like you, my dad doesn't need enemies."

"Don't presume to judge what you don't understand. Neither you nor my daughter ever showed the least interest in business. You have no idea how our world works."

"I know that my dad's world is one worth living in and yours isn't."

She wasn't surprised by the hangup that followed. Nor was she tempted to call back. Romi had gotten the information she'd wanted.

Maddie *had* made the threat. Whatever the particulars were, Romi didn't know and wasn't about to interrupt her SBC's honeymoon to find out.

Maddie hadn't told her because she knew Romi would have demanded she tear up the paperwork. To no avail. Romi had no doubts on that score.

Maddie could be more obdurate than executives in the oil industry denying the existence of global warming.

Even if Romi told Maddie of Max's threat, the redhead wouldn't alter the paperwork. In a month maybe, when she was happily married and sure that Viktor would keep a tight rein on Jeremy. But until then? Maddie would not consider losing the shares worth backing down from her father.

Oh, Romi planned to talk to her SBC about it anyway. When she got back from her honeymoon, but since the threat to her shares wasn't the main reason Romi planned to say *yes* to Max's proposal, it wasn't a priority.

She wasn't going to say yes because of his threat to her father's sobriety either. Harry Grayson wasn't going to *stay* sober if he couldn't remain in the program without the motivation of Max's merger. Romi was honest enough to admit to herself that she hoped this thing worked for her dad both in the short and long term, but she wasn't marrying Max and signing his ridiculously long prenuptial agreement for her dad's sake.

She was going to say yes to the blackmail proposal because she couldn't imagine her life without Max in it.

Did that mean she'd done the one thing she'd been determined not to and fallen in love with the Corporate Tsar?

She thought probably it did.

Surprisingly, that knowledge did not make her want to bury her head in the sand or run. In fact, there was a certain amount of freedom in acknowledging that there was no point in fighting something that had already happened.

She loved Maxwell Black and had every intention of taking a chance on marriage to him. Romi was primarily a positive person. She hoped for the best and for the most part believed it would come to pass.

She'd broken things off with Max a year ago because he had put a definitive sell-by date on their relationship.

There was nothing to hope for when he'd been adamant he only wanted six months to a year.

The prenup he'd given her to read over made it clear he didn't expect the marriage to last past ten years, but there was no *requirement* they divorce at that time. Regardless of the language of the contract, Max was going into this with a different attitude.

For one thing, he wanted children with her. Enough that he'd lost his vaunted control enough to make love to her without protection. Subconsciously, he wasn't afraid of creating that permanent bond between them.

After his own childhood, he wasn't *ever* walking away from his children, even if he thought he might walk away from her.

It might be wishful thinking, but Romi doubted that outcome, too.

A lifetime wouldn't be enough to grow bored or grow apart. They shared a soul even if he didn't see it that way and she thought maybe he was starting to get an inkling.

Romi had never been a person to be dictated by what others believed. *She* believed in soul mates and, she realized now, she believed Maxwell Black was hers.

How could she *not* take the chance on marriage to him?

When he came by for dinner, she'd have an overnight bag packed and an answer to his proposal.

CHAPTER TEN

MAXWELL CURSED THE tail end of rush-hour traffic as he drove toward the exclusive neighborhood where Harry Grayson had purchased his house before Romi had ever been born.

Maxwell would be cutting it fine, but he had every intention of arriving by the seven o'clock deadline.

If another lover had required an earlier time for dinner, he would have simply canceled. The fact he hadn't even considered doing so with Romi was somewhat disconcerting, but perhaps not so shocking.

He planned to make her his wife. That would require different concessions on his part.

The type of concessions he had made for no one but his mother and she rarely asked of him. He had no doubts Romi wouldn't be nearly as accommodating.

He might have no direct personal experience with that kind of thing, but Maxwell had always assumed a wife would be more demanding of his time and attention than any of his lovers.

Hence his lack of desire to ever enter the wedded state. Before this.

He wanted Romi, though. And she required more than a short-term affair. Though she'd tried to talk him into a one-night stand. For her *first* time.

He could not believe she'd thought a single night would be enough for them.

They were not just combustible in bed, he and Romi were an atom separating with nuclear force. Only they generated that kind of power when they came together.

The housekeeper led him into the living room, where Romi was sitting on the sofa looking through the same photo albums that had so fascinated him. Her father's drinking problem and loss of her mother aside, Romi had lived a clearly happy childhood.

The photographic evidence had shown that and so much more. Those albums revealed Harry Grayson's deep love for his daughter and for the woman he had married and lost.

Looking through them had made Maxwell question for the first time whether domestic bliss was truly an oxymoron.

Romi looked up when he came into the room, her gaze not quite focused, her thoughts clearly in the past. "Max. You're here."

"As you see," he replied wryly.

She smiled, her attention fixing more firmly on him. "On time. I'm impressed."

"You said seven."

"I did." She closed and stacked the albums. "I thought we could eat here before going back to your place."

So, she wasn't going to fight spending the night with him. Good.

The relief he felt in response to that knowledge was not acute. He was simply glad to avoid that particular argument.

They had more important things to do with their time. "I have reservations." At one of San Francisco's best restaurants.

It also happened to be one he knew Romi enjoyed.

Romi smiled at him persuasively. "Mrs. K made her famous spinach lasagna."

"Famous with whom?" he asked, not averse to the more private setting for their conversation.

Romi shrugged, self-deprecation in her tone. "Maddie and me."

"Then, by all means, I must taste this famous lasagna."

Romi's smile was blinding then and he made no effort to squelch the urge to kiss the happily curved lips.

Afterward, while Romi put away the photo albums, he called and canceled his reservations.

The table in the formal dining room was large enough for sixteen, but only one end was set, shrinking the large space to friendly dimensions. The white linen and candles set a tone that he hoped boded well for Romi's decision.

He pulled the light blue ring box out of his pocket and set it beside the place setting meant for Romi.

Her eyes tracked his movements, her expression for once not revealing even the smallest detail of what she was thinking. "I thought you were bringing that to dinner tomorrow."

"I will then, too, if that is necessary." But after last night, what were the chances Romi was really going to deny him?

Pretty low.

Maxwell spent his days assessing decisions just like this one and he rarely made a mistake. The emotional component existed in business as well.

The only true unknown entity was the way Romi's mind worked. Her reactions were guided by a set of rules he did not understand. He was still nearly one-hundred-percent sure of the outcome.

For one thing, there was the possibility, no matter how remote, that she was pregnant.

Ramona Grayson wasn't the type of woman to dismiss that as unimportant.

For another, she had wanted to give him her innocence. That was a gift of unparalleled importance in either of their worlds and would factor into her decision, even if she refused to acknowledge that truth to herself.

Romi didn't answer his implied question, but took her

seat. He joined her, unsurprised when Mrs. K came in with the salad course immediately.

"Tell me about your day," he said to Romi as he spread his napkin in his lap.

She didn't hesitate, opening up with frustrated candor about her phone call with Jeremy Archer. "He's just so cold."

"Business is all he knows."

Romi dismissed that with a wave of her hand, her fork thankfully empty. "Some people would the say the same about you, but you're not like him."

"You don't think so?" he asked, surprised by the observation.

He and the president of AIH had a lot in common. Though Maxwell was better at business than the older man. His killer instincts were more refined and his focus wasn't caught up with how he looked to others. Maxwell did whatever the hell he wanted and didn't worry if old-money San Francisco business approved.

Romi's expression took on a rare implacability. "You wouldn't make your daughter the pawn in a business proposal."

"No." Though how Romi had realized that truth in the face of what he *would* do, he couldn't quite figure.

Maxwell shook his head.

"What?"

"You don't make sense to me," he admitted.

"So you've said."

Touché. "One day I'm going to figure you out."

"Good luck with that. *I'm* not always sure why I do or think the things I do." She winked and gave him a wry smile.

Now, that did *not* surprise him. "Archer and I both do whatever we need to get what we want."

"No. You've already admitted you wouldn't use your child, so you don't do *whatever*. You do what you think is expedient and gives you the most control."

She, on the other hand, understood *him* all too well.

"Some things are easier to control than others," he informed her.

"You mean like people."

"Yes." Like her.

"Like me," she said, echoing his thoughts.

"Like you." It was something he was only beginning to come to terms with.

"Good. I don't think I could consider marrying you if that weren't true."

He'd never considered his inability to control her would be a benefit where she was concerned. He should have. Which only showed how off his usual game he was when it came to Ramona Grayson.

He had to admit, if only to himself, he enjoyed the fact she was so difficult to pin down as well.

Regardless, he already knew she was considering his proposal; he wanted to know if she was going to accept it. "Have you come to any conclusions?"

"I'm going to turn down the director position for LZO."

Okay, not what he'd been asking, but she knew that. "What is LZO?"

"A start-up environmental group."

"And you're turning down the directorship why?" He would have thought that kind of thing fit Romi to a *T*.

Romi waited to answer until she'd eaten another bite and taken a sip of her Australian Shiraz. "Maddie and I are starting a charter school for kids that need a break."

"I didn't know that." And it chagrined him that he didn't.

"Viktor is buying us a building as a wedding gift for Maddie. With the income from her trust and my Grayson inheritance and savings, we can swing operating expenses until we get the donor roll established."

"I thought environmentalism was your thing." Maxwell didn't examine his annoyance at the thought of Viktor feeding Romi's dream, even if it was one she shared with the man's wife.

"And children. It's all about making the world a better place for the generations to come, right?"

He wasn't sure, but he liked the outlook. "I'm impressed."

"Thanks."

"I will dedicate fifty percent of BIT's corporate giving to the school on a yearly basis." He didn't need to take time to think about it.

He believed in giving back and not because he was a bleeding heart like Romi, but there were very few charitable options Maxwell felt a personal connection to. Anything related to Romi would be one of them.

Romi gasped. "That's…" She trailed off, clearly speechless.

"About three million a year." And better than a building, even if the building cost more up front.

"I don't know what to say."

"Say yes."

"It's reliant on me marrying you?" she asked.

He couldn't tell if the idea disappointed or upset her. Maxwell didn't know what to think of this new ability to hide her emotions from him. He didn't like it, though.

He shook his head, making an instant decision and taking a gamble. "No, Romi. I believe in the next generation, too."

Which was nothing but the truth.

She stared at him, like she was trying to read his sincerity.

He lifted his brow in query. "Do you want it in writing before you give me your decision?"

"No." She ducked her head as Mrs. K brought in their dinner plates.

When the housekeeper was gone, Romi looked up at him. "I believe you."

She might think she didn't trust him, but she did. And

his risk had paid off because he'd made her realize it, even if only a little.

"Thank you." Her words were soft, but the look in her eyes?

Pure hero worship.

And he loved it.

"You are welcome," he replied. "I will have my corporate-giving coordinator contact you next week."

"Actually, we've got a lot of paperwork to fill out, permits to file, et cetera, before we're a fully functioning nonprofit."

No doubt. "I have someone who can help you with that."

"Maddie was going to use her trust's lawyers."

"The school's financial picture will look better with a lawyer that doesn't charge fifteen hundred an hour." The old-money lawyers in San Francisco didn't do pro bono and they charged three times as much as decent corporate lawyers with less prestigious clientele and addresses.

"True."

"I'll text you the firm's name and contact information. I'll let them know to expect your call."

"I'll talk to Maddie about it when she gets back from her honeymoon."

"Palm Springs? What kind of honeymoon is that?" He liked the city himself, but it was hardly the exotic locale most would consider for a wealthy businessman and his heiress wife's honeymoon.

"One tailored to the woman who loves that city above all others."

"Really?"

"It holds good memories for her."

"What about you?"

Romi shrugged. "I like it. She and I have been there together many times."

Was his soon-to-be fiancée being deliberately obtuse? "Is it *your* ideal honeymoon spot?"

"Not really." One of Romi's charming blushes pinkened her cheeks.

Intriguing. "Where would you want to go?"

"Europe would be nice."

"But not where you were thinking of. Come on, *milaya*, spill."

She bit her lip and then sighed. "Building a house with one of the organizations that provide homes for people and families in need. You know, something like that. Something we could look back on and say we started our lives together giving a family a home."

Okay. That was unexpected.

"We could not simply buy a house for some deserving family?" he asked faintly, excitement not his first reaction to the idea.

"It's not the same, is it?" Romi asked. She shrugged dismissively. "It doesn't matter. Just a dream. We wouldn't have a honeymoon anyway."

"Why not?" He really didn't understand the way her mind worked.

Didn't Romi want a honeymoon?

She shrugged again and then looked down at her dinner, cutting a precise bite of the lasagna. "I mean, it's not like we're a romantic couple."

They were something and it wasn't a couple who was going to skip their honeymoon.

"Madison and Viktor are?" he asked with sarcasm.

Romi's head snapped up and her eyes were filled with fervor. "They are. I mean, they both act like it's all about the deal and protecting Maddie's reputation and our dream for the charter school while Viktor gets to take over AIH, but they're so in love it's sickening."

"Are you sure you aren't seeing things that aren't there?" Maxwell's old friend had looked besotted at the wedding and reception, though.

"No. They'll both figure it out eventually. Until then,

things are going to be a little tense. You know with the whole, 'you married me to get my dad's company' thing between them."

"Maybe Archer was just playing matchmaker."

"I don't think so." Romi grimaced. "He offered the contract to you, too."

Romi really didn't like Jeremy Archer.

"Madison was never going to consider anyone but Viktor."

"Her dad didn't know that."

"Maybe he did." Archer wasn't an idiot after all.

"Yeah, you go on believing that."

"You hold a grudge, don't you?"

Romi looked surprised. "Actually, it takes a lot to make me mad, but then…yes, I suppose it takes a *lot* more to change that. And I'm really protective of the people I love."

"I've noticed."

"Yes, well…"

"It's an admirable trait. I, too, am protective of the people important to me." His list was just much, much shorter.

Up to the point he'd met Romi, it had had one name on it. Natalya Black.

He thought Romi probably had quite a few friends that had tasted her fierce loyalty, even if they weren't as close to her as Harry Grayson or Madison Beck.

Romi dropped all pretense of eating and met his gaze, her own beautiful blue eyes filled with serious lights. "Would your wife be important to you?"

Relieved that he could admit to the uncommon protectiveness without acknowledging whatever nebulous feelings might drive it, he nodded. "Naturally."

"At least as long as we're married."

He considered her words and how wrong they felt. "I think that once we have been married, you will always be on my short list of those who can claim my protection."

Provided the divorce was amicable, but he'd never had

a bad breakup. Of course just the thought of Romi walking away from him annoyed Maxwell.

Not something they had to discuss right now however. "Tell me about building houses in Haiti."

"It could be anywhere in the world really, but Maddie and I did it three summers in a row in Mexico. We always said we wanted to participate in a Haiti build, though."

"I'm having a hard time picturing Madcap Madison and Romi Grayson, well-known activist heiress, building houses in the Mexican heat."

"It was the most amazing experience. Everyone works like dogs to get these really simple dwellings built in a week, but the families are so grateful. The children…they're incredible. I loved working with them even more than working on the house team."

He could well imagine and said so.

She smiled, mischief glinting in her gaze. "You know what I can't imagine?"

"What?"

"You pouring concrete in the Haitian sun wearing scrubs and a sun hat."

Neither could he. Surely he could wear something else.

She must have read his look because she laughed. "Some people wear jeans and long-sleeved T-shirts, but scrubs are the most comfortable. They let air circulate and are easy to get clean. Both are important."

He wondered if his tailor did scrubs. "I see."

"So, what about you?"

"What about me?" He'd never had dreams of building a house in Haiti, that was for sure.

"What would your ideal honeymoon be?"

He liked that she asked, so he told her the truth. "I would like to visit Russia, meet the family that turned their backs on my mother and show them the success she raised without their help."

"I bet they regret pushing her away and miss her."

"If they do, they've never contacted her to say so."

Romi frowned. "Maybe they don't know how. Did she tell them she was emigrating to the United States?"

"I do not know."

"She changed her name, right?"

"Yes."

"So, neither of you would have been easy to find."

He refused to let them off the hook of responsibility so easily. "Where there is a will, there is a way."

"For men like you? Absolutely. For lesser mortals, not so much."

He didn't want to discuss his mother's estranged family any longer. He didn't even consider them his relatives. "Tell me you made your decision."

"I won't say I don't care about Maddie's shares."

"But…" he offered, because her tone implied it.

Damn. Was she going to say *no?* He did not believe it.

She fiddled with her silverware, looking down at the table before meeting his gaze, her own filled with certainty. "And you know how important my dad's health is to me."

"Yes."

"*But* I won't let you use either to blackmail me into marriage."

"You won't." A flurry of curse words fought to come out of his mouth. Maxwell bit them back.

Romi reached out and picked up the ring box. "So, you're going to have to deal with the fact that I'm agreeing because I can't imagine living the rest of my life without you in it."

Everything inside of Maxwell went still. "What?"

Romi's gaze warmed with emotion he refused to name. "I will marry you."

Totally unexpected and extremely unfamiliar panic filled him. "I don't love you. I won't love you." Double damn. Why did his code of honor insist on rearing its head right now?

"So you've said."

"And you are okay with that?" he asked, his mouth spilling words his brain had not authorized.

"Does it matter?"

She should ask. He'd been willing to give her compelling motivation to do what he wanted.

But this…this offer of herself because she wanted to do it? He had no frame of reference for it, zero sense of control with it.

"It does," he admitted shortly.

"You don't sound happy about that."

"I don't like the rules of the game to change."

"Unless you're the one doing the changing?"

"That goes without saying."

"I'll sign the prenup," she offered, like a lollipop to a crying child.

He frowned. "Yes, you will."

She grinned. "Feel better?"

"I did not *feel* badly to begin with. You are accepting my deal, whatever your reasons." That was exactly what he wanted.

"Yes, I am."

Why did he feel like that was entirely on her terms and because it was what *she* wanted? She'd agreed to sign the prenup. She'd agreed to the marriage. His plan had led to exactly the outcome he wanted, but somehow it had become her plan, too.

Was that what it meant to marry rather than take a lover? No other woman had ever influenced Maxwell's plans.

He sipped his wine, almost enjoying the sense of being off-kilter. It was so foreign to him. Maybe when the source was the woman who had blown his mind in bed the night before, it wasn't such a bad thing.

"I told your father I was going to marry you," Maxwell informed her.

Romi cast Maxwell a wary glance. "You were right."

"He seemed to think it would only happen if you wanted it to."

Romi grinned. "He was right, too."

For the first time in adult memory, Maxwell did not know what to say. She had chosen him even though he didn't love her like her father had loved her mother. What did that mean? Did she see an expiration date on their relationship?

Was the sex that good?

Did she plan to find the love of her life *after* Maxwell? Anger washed over him at the idea.

Romi handed him the Tiffany box.

He took it with a silent question.

"I'd like to tell our children about the moment their father proposed."

That did not sound like a woman planning to move on to someone else later. Still, he couldn't let her think this was a romantic moment between two people who believed in forever. "I am not going on one knee."

"Fine." She stared at him expectantly, the vibrant blue of her eyes glowing with it.

"You already agreed to marry me."

"Yes." She sighed, some of the expectation dimming and along with it the glow. "Do you really want me to put the ring on myself?"

"No!" Damn. Where had *that* come from?

Her expression lightened and only then did he realize hurt had begun to shadow her blue gaze. That's where the glow had gone.

The Russian curse words that flowed through his mind in that moment put the others to shame.

He stood and moved around the table until he stood beside her chair. Leaning down, he gripped the back of the chair and turned it so she faced him.

Her eyes had gone round, her mouth dropping open in surprise. "Max?"

"There should be a story for our children." Russians understood family stories, the history that really mattered.

It wasn't about promising love for a lifetime.

He dropped to one knee, flipped the ring box open and offered it to Romi. "Will you marry me, Ramona Grayson?"

Beautiful blue eyes glistening suspiciously, she nodded her head really fast.

"Words, *dorogaya*. Give me the words. For your children." And for him, though he would never say so.

"Yes, Maxwell Black, I will marry you and I don't care how airtight that book you call a prenuptial agreement is, you'll have a heck of a time getting rid of me."

He didn't argue with her. Maxwell didn't want to dwell on invoking the clauses in the contract.

He took the ring from the box and put his hand out imperiously for hers. She gave it to him without hesitation, placing her left hand into his.

He slid the custom-designed engagement ring onto her finger and only then did she look down at it.

The ten-karat blue sapphire was the same shade as her eyes, the large diamonds on either side sparkling with Romi's effervescence. Set in a vintage-style Russian gold filigree band, he was very pleased with the Tiffany master jeweler's design.

"It's beautiful," she said in an emotion-laden voice.

"I had it designed for you."

"You're a planner."

"I am." No need to tell her the designers had been working on the ring since well before Jeremy Archer's marriage contract offer for his daughter.

"It's really big."

"But it fits you." And he didn't mean the size. Naturally, he'd gotten that right.

She choked out a laugh. "It does. I should be all about how ostentatious it is, but I love it."

"It sparkles like you do."

"Ooh, you really do say some of the cheesiest things and make them sound way too romantic."

He shrugged. "It's a gift."

That had only manifested for this woman, but who was keeping track?

"Are you ready to go home?" he asked.

Romi's face contorted with emotion. "Other than college dorms, I've never lived anywhere but here."

"You like the penthouse."

"I do."

"But this is home."

"Dad needed me for so long, I couldn't think of living anywhere else."

"Even so, you love this house, don't you?"

Romi nodded but smiled as she stood, no reluctance evident in her manner. "I'm ready to go."

They hadn't finished dinner, but he didn't think either of them was worried about that right now.

He wanted to go back to the penthouse and consummate Romi's promise to be his and he was certain she wanted the same.

CHAPTER ELEVEN

KNOWING MAX WOULD want it as much as she did, Romi had packed for a much longer stay than overnight.

Triumph had flashed in his gaze when he'd seen her suitcases and matching carryall. He'd smiled, too. "Lime green with white polka dots?"

"I suppose your luggage is black."

"No." He winked. "It's brown leather."

She melted at the wink and poured herself into the passenger seat of his growling predator of a car.

He shocked her by insisting she unpack before doing anything else, but when her last pair of bright purple jeans was hanging in his walk-in closet, which was the size of a small bedroom—and empty on one side for her—he carried her off to bed and they made love.

She'd thought maybe the night before had been so beyond the known universe because it was her first time, but she'd soon discovered it was just being with this man.

He rocked her world and by every indication she did the same for him.

Maddie returned from her honeymoon in high spirits and ready to find a building for the charter school. She and Romi spent hours trailing after Viktor's incredibly competent Realtor.

Not really sure why she did it, Romi hid her engagement ring in her purse whenever they were together. She didn't tell her SBC that Romi's father was in rehab and Romi herself was living with the man she intended to marry.

"Would you like to have Madison and Viktor over?" Max asked as she curled into his side while they watched his favorite crime drama one evening after Maddie's return to town.

They shared similar taste in music and most television shows. Their workout regimens were complementary and they had the same favorite area restaurants.

But she wasn't a huge fan of the crime drama they were watching, so she'd been texting with Maddie while it played.

"Huh? What?"

He turned down the television, a one-hundred-and-twenty-eight-inch screen that dropped down from the ceiling. "I said, you should invite Viktor and Madison over for dinner."

No, he'd asked if she wanted to. Apparently, to Max it was the same thing. "Uh…"

"We'll have it catered if you like."

Romi actually liked Max's housekeeper's cooking. She was no Mrs. K, but the woman was really talented at dinners that did well straight from the fridge or with an easy reheat. "That's not…I mean…Maddie doesn't know about us."

Max gave her ring a disbelieving look. "How can she not?"

"I…uh…I didn't tell her?"

"Are you asking me, or telling me?"

"Telling you."

"How did she miss the ring?" he asked, his tone carefully neutral.

"Um…I took it off."

Max picked up the remote and pressed a button. The television turned off and the screen lifted slowly toward the ceiling with a soft whir.

"Was your program over?" Romi asked, pretty sure it hadn't been, but she hadn't been paying attention.

"No."

"Oh, um…"

"That's a lot of ums for a woman who rarely feels the need for the word."

She didn't have an answer for that. He was right, she wasn't used to stumbling over her words.

He turned so their gazes caught. "Why haven't you told your sister-by-choice that you are engaged to be married and living with your fiancé?" Max's lips thinned and he did not sound happy.

"I…"

"You are not thinking about backing out."

"No."

"You said you wanted this."

"I do." Couldn't he tell how much she enjoyed being with him?

Dark gray eyes narrowed. "Then why?"

"They just got back from their honeymoon." It sounded lame, even to her own ears.

He wasn't impressed, either. "Nearly two weeks ago."

Romi had been hiding her ring and new living situation for weeks? It hadn't seemed that long. "Maddie is still settling into being married, though."

"And you sharing your own plans would somehow impede that?" Disbelief laced his tone.

"No. I don't know." Romi didn't really know why she didn't want to tell Maddie about Max.

"Viktor knows."

"What?" Romi demanded, sitting up in agitation. "How?"

"I told him."

"Why would you?"

"We are friends. More to the point why *wouldn't* you?"

"I…" Romi's gaze skittered around the room, seeking inspiration.

She'd discovered her whole avoidance thing didn't work with Max. Not only was he like a pit bull with a meaty bone when it came to discussing stuff he thought was important, but she also found herself wanting, even needing to deal with the real stuff when that real stuff included him.

Only not when it came to telling her SBC apparently.

"She's going to have to know or how will you ask her to be your matron of honor?" Max asked reasonably.

"For a courthouse wedding?" That was one thing Romi hadn't been worried about. "That's a little over-the-top."

He frowned. "Who said we were getting married in a courthouse?"

"Where else would we get married?"

"Holy Virgin Cathedral." His tone said he didn't understand why that hadn't been obvious to her.

"What? I thought…it's a business thing for you."

"It's a marriage and we're having a traditional Russian wedding. Mama is coming over tomorrow evening to discuss plans."

"Tomorrow?" Had he lost his mind? "No. That's impossible."

"Are you backing out?" he asked again.

"No!" Where did he get his ideas? "I told you I wasn't having second thoughts. It's just, I barely know your mother."

"All the more reason to have her for dinner. You can invite Madison and Viktor to join us."

"Get off the invite-them-to-dinner kick. When were you going to tell me your mother was coming?"

"I just did."

"That's not what I meant."

He made a visible grab for patience. "Romi, my mother wishes to get to know you."

"She's already met me."

"And yet you barely know her," he said, throwing her words back at her.

"Fine. So, she's coming for dinner. I'm not inviting Maddie."

"Why not?"

Romi thought about it, even as the sheer panic going through her did not abate, and realized she could think of no better buffer for this dinner with her future mother-in-law than her SBC.

Darn it. "She's going to be mad I didn't tell her." Really mad.

And Romi wouldn't blame her SBC, not even a little. She should have said something. Romi didn't understand why it was so hard for her, but she wasn't backing out and that meant telling Maddie about her upcoming marriage.

"She'll forgive you."

"I'm not ready to tell her."

He didn't ask why, just waited for her to say something.

"I always said I'd only marry a man who loved me as much as my dad loved my mom."

"I know," Max replied warily, like love was this really scary topic that could get up and bite him.

"She's going to think you love me."

"Is that a bad thing?"

"It's a lie." And Romi didn't want to lie to Maddie, but she wasn't willing to tell her SBC the truth, either.

That Romi was marrying a man she loved with every fiber of her being but who didn't believe in the emotion.

"What are you planning to do then? Wait to tell her when our first child is on the way?" Max asked with no small amount of exasperation. "I'm pretty sure Viktor will spill the beans before that."

"We aren't planning to get pregnant right away. We agreed."

"I was being facetious."

"Well, don't." Humor wasn't registering right now.

Max sighed and scooted closer, pulling Romi into his arms. "Madison married Viktor for reasons unrelated to love. She is not going to judge you."

"I know, but she won't understand, either. I'm not being

coerced." Even if Max had done his best to put the blackmail bid on the table.

He was silent for a few seconds and then he asked, "Does she know Harry is undergoing treatment for his alcoholism?"

"No."

"Don't you think she deserves to?"

"Yes, of course she does."

"So, tell her."

"It's not so easy."

"Why not?"

"Because I'm waiting for you to change your mind," she burst out and then covered her mouth with her hand, shocked by her own words.

"About what?" he asked. "The merger with Grayson Enterprises is a done deal. Your dad isn't leaving the treatment facility."

"That's not what I'm worried about."

"What then?"

"What if you decide you don't want to marry me?" she asked, stunned as the words revealed the worries she hadn't realized were plaguing her.

Max didn't look shocked. He looked patient. Aargh.

"Romi, *dorogaya*, I am the one who blackmailed you. Remember?" He tugged until she was straddling his lap.

She pressed close. "I like it when you call me that, not just in the bedroom."

"I will remember as you should how you came to be wearing my ring and it was not some great feminine plot that I'm going to wiggle out of soon."

"Right." Because they'd already signed the prenup and applied for the license.

Only she was getting almost everything she'd ever dreamed of. She was marrying the man of her dreams. They were planning a family together. Her dad was on his way to healthy. It was all so good, she was terrified everything was going to fall apart.

"You are mine, *dorogaya*. I am not letting you go."

She wanted to believe that. So much. "I thought we were just waiting to get married until my dad was out of treatment." At the courthouse. No fanfare.

Fanfare. A church wedding. That all just made it real. And real things could be destroyed or lost.

"We are."

"But you want a big wedding."

"Yes."

"At the church."

"Naturally."

"So, we have to set a date." She knew that only a *significant* donation to the restoration fund had gotten Maddie and Viktor their wedding date.

"Yes."

"Your mother wants to help plan the wedding."

"I am her only child."

"I haven't had a mother in six years." And her dad was in no condition to plan a wedding.

Though she very much wanted him to give her away.

Max cocked his head to one side. "I thought Jenna died when you were three."

"She did, but Madison's mom took over. Helene Archer was my mother like Maddie is my sister."

"By choice."

"Yes. She loved me."

"Mama will adore you as well."

"Chance would be a fine thing." It was another thing her friend Kim from the U.K. said.

Sometimes those Britishisms were more fitting than anything else she could think to say.

He laughed. The jerk. Was still laughing.

"Stop. It's not funny."

"This panic? Is hilarious. My mother will adore you. Madison will be thrilled for you. We *will* be married."

"Oh." She blinked up at him, biting her lower lip. "Maybe you could say it again."

"We will be married in exactly five weeks, three days."

"What? You said we were waiting for my dad."

"He'll get a day pass and we'll have a dry reception."

"You would do that for him?"

Max rolled his eyes. "Where is all this coming from?"

"I don't know." The knowledge she was falling deeper and deeper in love every day and he was just as committed today as he'd been a year ago to keeping that emotion out of his repertoire?

Max tugged her into his lap and tilted her face up toward his with a hand under chin. "You are mine, Ramona Grayson. You can't take that promise back. We will marry in the cathedral and proclaim this truth before our friends and family."

"Doesn't sound much like a business arrangement."

"I am at heart still a Russian man."

"So, you have a soul even if you are a corporate shark."

"I thought tsar?" he teased.

"That, too. Maybe they're the same."

"Could be. Some of the tsars were known for their bloodthirsty ruthlessness."

"You are ruthless." And why *that* didn't scare her when the happiness within her grasp did was one of life's little mysteries.

"But you are in my circle of protection."

"So, I have nothing to fear from you."

"No."

If only that were true. "I love you, Max."

Sometimes, she just had to say it out loud. Though, come to think of it, this might be the first time she'd said those three little words to him.

The way he stopped moving and talking and just stared

at her indicated that might actually be the case. She said, "I do, you know."

"You did say you couldn't imagine your life without me in it."

Which was as good as an admission. "Yes, I did."

"I will treasure your love."

"Will you?" How could he if he thought it was a weak emotion.

"It is a gift I will not take for granted."

"Even if you can't return it."

He winced. "Yes."

"Okay."

"So, tell your SBC."

"I will."

"Good."

He sealed her promise with his lips.

She returned the kiss with enthusiasm, helping him when nimble masculine fingers began unbuttoning the oversized tie-dyed men's-style dress shirt worn with her leggings.

His Armani sweater was an easy tug and off, and then there was just the black silk T-shirt, which followed with a ripple of his muscles.

She explored his chest, rubbing her body against his. This was always good. No matter when, how often or what they did together, it was good. Better than good. Incredible.

Their sexual compatibility couldn't be questioned. So, why couldn't he take the next step and love her?

If he wanted to know why she didn't want to have dinner with his mother? Maybe it was because Romi would rather smack the woman for teaching Max to eschew love in favor of pragmatism and carefully cultivated ruthlessness.

He showed that ruthlessness now, teasing Romi to the point of whimpering need, before lifting her and sliding her onto his condom-covered erection. She was on top, but he drove the coupling, thrusting up into her and hitting that spot inside that made fireworks go off inside Romi's head.

He held her hips in place, controlling the depth and angle of his thrusts.

They never broke eye contact through the long minutes of coupling and intense pleasure. She saw the way his skin flushed with the increased blood pressure that came before climax.

He could easily see the way her hair grew damp around her face from perspiration.

Bottomless pools, dark and mysterious, his eyes bored into hers, speaking messages she couldn't decipher, but that increased her bliss all the same.

She'd learned to appreciate the scent of his desire and even more so their combined musk. It was a heady fragrance that added to her desire, but also her security in their intimacy.

This was theirs alone. No one else combined with him for the exact same perfume of lust.

The way he inhaled deeply showed he enjoyed it just as much.

"My love," she gasped as her body hovered on the precipice of ultimate pleasure.

That dark gaze flared with something intense and his thrusting grew stronger and erratic.

"You like that word," she said with wonder.

"On your lips."

But not on his own. She refused to let that dampen the moment between them.

She simply reveled in the joy of intimacy and how much he clearly liked knowing he owned her heart.

"You are mine," he said, reflecting her thoughts.

"You are mine, too." She needed them both to acknowledge that fact.

"Yes."

She nodded, satisfaction and pleasure warring for supremacy in her heart. "With no expiration date."

He didn't reply, just increased his pace, his expression so intent, it sent shivers throughout her oversensitized body.

With knowing fingers, he shifted her and changed his own angle so his pelvic bone pressed into her pleasure spot on every upward piston of his hips.

Mini explosions of delight accompanied each movement, pleasure spiraling inside until it released in a cataclysm that made her scream and bow her body in shattering ecstasy.

They were cuddled in the bed after their shower, his body an octopus around her like she'd grown accustomed to, her breathing even and shallow as she hovered at the edge of sleep.

"You are mine," he whispered into her hair. "No expirations."

It was a huge admission, even if he made it when he thought she'd already fallen under the influence of the sandman.

Maddie took the news of Romi's engagement way better than she expected. "I thought there was something between you and that guy."

"Something big."

"You love him."

"I do."

"It's catching."

"So, you finally admitted it to yourself?" Romi asked her SBC.

"I did." She glowed with the kind of happiness Romi had rarely witnessed in her life. "He loves me, too."

"Oh, honey. That's wonderful. I mean I knew it, I just didn't know he'd admit it so quickly." Romi ignored the flicker of regret that she couldn't say the same, her genuine joy for her SBC big enough to cover it easily.

"Yeah, well something happened with my dad."

"Tell me about it," Romi demanded.

"He threatened to have me committed...to stop me from

taking control of my inheritance from the Madison Trust when I turn twenty-five."

Romi was shocked. Even Jeremy Archer wasn't that awful. "That jerk!"

"That's kind of what I thought."

Romi experienced a guilty twinge. "I think I know why he made the threat."

"Why?" Maddie asked.

"Because I asked him about the paperwork you signed that spelled out my dad would get the shares to AIH in the Madison Family Trust once you gained control in a couple of weeks."

"How did you find out about it?"

"Max told me."

"Oh." Maddie didn't look too worried, definitely no inkling Max might have used the situation as leverage with Romi. "I don't know why that would set my dad off. I mean he knows half the shares are going to you regardless."

"Max didn't tell me that!"

"Why not, I wonder?"

"Anyway, only my dad would have triggered the shares going to your dad. So, unless he wanted to take over Grayson Enterprises, his shares were safe. I didn't think he wanted the company that badly."

"Even if he did, it wasn't going to happen. My dad and Max signed a merger contract. Grayson Enterprises is now a subsidiary of BIT."

"That's great. He's protecting you already."

That was one way to look at it. Was in fact how Romi chose to see Max's actions. "He got Dad to go into treatment."

Maddie's eyes filled with tears and she hugged Romi. "I'm so glad, sweetie."

"Me, too." But something about what Maddie said had Romi thinking.

"So your dad was the only one who could trigger the

share dump from the trust?" Romi asked, trying to understand.

"Yes. I was protecting your dad's company from him."

"But…" That wasn't what Max had said.

To be fair, he could have misunderstood. Unlikely, but possible.

Not that it mattered. Romi hadn't made her decision about marrying him because of the shares.

"Wait a minute, you're giving me half of your shares?" she asked as that fact registered completely.

No. No way.

"Yeah, but you and I both know you'll just put the money back into the school. My dad needed to understand that he couldn't threaten you with impunity." Maddie so clearly didn't care about the wealth involved.

Romi was appalled. "But he threatened to have you committed."

"That was never going to happen." Maddie sounded so confident. "I'm not mentally fragile and even if he could get that self-serving doctor to say I was, Vik would never have let him get away with it."

"It's nice to know you have backup, isn't it?" Romi wasn't sure Maxwell Black would be as protective of her as Viktor Beck was of Maddie, but she knew he had her back in a way no one other than Maddie had in too many years to think about.

His deal with her dad showed that, no matter what justifications Max put on it.

"Yes. We've always been there for each other, but for a long time, we didn't have the power." Maddie was obviously as pleased by the turn their lives had taken as Romi was.

Romi's smile was still wry. "Not being corporate sharks in the making and all."

"It's…I'm…I'm just so happy," Maddie said, sounding a little flabbergasted by that reality.

Romi hugged her again. "And I'm incredibly happy for you."

"Ditto, sis, ditto."

Maddie assumed Romi was marrying for love and Romi let her keep thinking that. She'd spent her life protecting the people she loved and she wasn't going to stop now.

Besides, it wasn't a lie. Romi *was* marrying Max because she loved him and that was a truth that covered pretty much everything else.

"So, you'll come to dinner?" she pressed Maddie.

Her SBC nodded firmly. "Of course we will."

"Good. Max's mom is going to be there."

"She'll love you. How can she help herself?"

Romi laughed. "You're biased."

"Family should be." Maddie's grin was conspiratorial.

And Romi returned it in kind. "Yes, they should be."

Neither mentioned how that *didn't* work with Jeremy Archer.

CHAPTER TWELVE

"Did you make this, Ramona?" Natalya asked Maxwell's fiancée.

Romi shook her head. "I'm afraid not."

His mama looked up at him with a fond smile. "Did you cook, *mishka?*"

"No, *Mama*. We ordered in."

"Oh." She frowned. "Ramona does not cook?"

"She's too busy saving the world," Madison said with a laugh.

His mother turned her attention to Viktor's wife. "Yes? I would think something might be left over for home."

"Mama," Max said in a tone he knew would get her attention. "I am not marrying Romi for her cooking skills. I employ a housekeeper for a reason and have more than one catering service on call."

"Well, yes, of course."

"Too bad Mrs. K won't be coming with Romi. That woman is a domestic goddess, but the only person she's more committed to taking care of than Romi is Harry," Madison said with a smile.

"She's besotted, but he'll never see it." Romi's laugh was a welcome sound.

She'd grown increasingly brittle in his mother's company. He didn't know why Natalya was behaving like this, but he was beginning to question the wisdom of asking her to help plan the wedding.

Madison nodded. "It's too bad, too."

"Can you imagine my father and Mrs. K?" Romi asked with still overflowing amusement.

"You believe your father should not consider his domestic staff in a romantic way?" his mother asked with some bite.

Maxwell stifled the urge to roll his eyes.

"Under most circumstances, it would be very bad form," Romi said with no give in her tone. "Making a pass at one's employees is not acceptable behavior and my father has too much honor to do such a thing."

"Does he?" Natalya asked, sounding unconvinced.

Maxwell wondered how long before he could offer to take her home. She did not like to drive and preferred his company over a car and driver.

"Yes," Romi replied with exaggerated patience. "But in this case, I'm sure Mrs. K would welcome his interest."

"She's a law unto herself," Madison agreed. "Mrs. K would run rings around him and I don't think she'd give up her job."

Maxwell's mother sniffed. "Surely she would be happy to keep home for him as his wife rather than housekeeper."

Instead of looking even a little offended, Romi's expression turned thoughtful. "You know, Natalya, I believe you are right. She might just keep him on the straight and narrow, too."

"Matchmaking thoughts?" Madison teased.

Romi made no effort to deny it. "I can't believe I didn't think of it before."

"You wanted the best for Mrs. K and your dad was too lost in his grief and the bottle to be that." Madison showed none of Romi's tendency to ignore the tougher subjects.

Romi considered her friend's words. "He still could be… lost in his grief."

"No. He's going to get better and come out of this treatment stronger. I just know it," Madison said with certainty. "Right, Vik?"

Viktor nodded. "I am sure you are right."

He didn't even sound a little like he was just humoring his wife. The besotted look he gave her however, put anything he said in agreement under the light of suspicion.

The man had succumbed and there was no doubt about it.

"Alcoholism is a genetic trait," Natalya pointed out with overt significance and a complete lack of tact.

Romi flinched and Maxwell stood without thought. "*Mam*, I will call for the car. Please gather your things."

"What, *mishka?* What do you mean? I am not finished with my dinner." She pointed to her only half-eaten plate.

He did not care. "You are."

"I was just pointing out that you might not be choosing from the strongest gene pool for your future progeny," she said as if that should make her thoughtless words acceptable.

The look he gave his mother was one he could never remember turning on her. "Romi is the woman I am going to marry, the only woman I have *ever* considered having children with and the only one I ever will."

"I didn't say—"

"I know exactly what you said and so does everyone here. If you hope for an invitation to return, you will apologize to Romi before we leave."

"But, my son—"

"What does *mishka* mean?" Romi asked, apropos of nothing.

At least in Maxwell's viewpoint.

"Little bear, though there's nothing little about my son," his mother answered, appearing as confused as Maxwell felt. "It is a childhood nickname that stuck."

Maxwell winced. Only with her had the nickname stuck and she only used it when she was reminding him that he would always be her son.

Romi's smile was too sweet in the current situation. "I like it."

Maxwell stared between the two women. His mother was

staring at Romi with an unexpected measure of respect. What had just happened?

Maxwell looked around the table to see if the others seemed to have more of a clue than he did. Viktor gave him a commiserating look tinged by clear confusion.

It was good to know Maxwell wasn't alone in his reaction to Romi.

Madison didn't look bewildered at all. Romi's sister-by-choice looked ready to strangle his mother.

And he couldn't blame her.

"I apologize if what I said offended you," his mother offered to Romi with the first sign of real warmth that evening.

"It did, but then I consider the source." Romi's words took a second to register for both Maxwell and his mother.

She gasped, but instead of getting angry as he expected, she smiled. "Touché. He is my baby, even if he is a business tycoon."

"Corporate Tsar. It's more fitting, don't you think?" Romi asked, no anger in her tone.

"He can be very imperious." Natalya looked at him with an expression that said maybe he was being that right now.

"I'm sure he doesn't get it from a stranger." Romi's smile took some of the sting from her words, but not all. "There's more than one flaw floating in our gene pool I guess."

Incredibly, his mother laughed.

Romi reached out, took his wrist and tugged. "Sit down, Mr. Tsar. Your mom will behave and we've got wedding plans to make."

"Your fiancée is a very confusing woman," his mother said. "I like her."

"I do, too. Very much."

"More than that, I think," Viktor said with that smug superiority Maxwell always wanted to knock off is his face.

Surprisingly, Mama didn't start in on one of her antilove tirades. She was busy asking Madison where she thought they should go shopping for Romi's wedding gown.

"I've asked our favorite boutique to get in a selection of vintage bohemian chic."

"You are not going to wear your mother's gown?" Viktor had asked what Maxwell wanted to.

Admittedly, he knew little of this type of thing, but Jeremy Archer had happily proclaimed to anyone who would listen that Madison was wearing her mother's wedding dress.

"Maddie's dress is a family heirloom," Romi explained. "My mom's was a typical 1980s monstrosity. Poufy sleeves, layers and layers of polyester lace and about four inches too long for me."

"Oh," Max said as if he'd asked the question.

"It's really not Romi at all. Besides, her dad doesn't need the reminder," Madison declared.

Romi grimaced and Maxwell reached down to squeeze her thigh in support. "He will be delighted to see you in your finery, whatever it ends up being."

Her smile in appreciation of his support was worth any amount of firm talks he would have to have with his mother.

"Where are we having the reception?" Natalya asked.

"We will host it, it's the bride's family's prerogative," Madison replied with no room for question.

"You and the Graysons are related?" Mama asked.

"She's my sister-by-choice," Madison said firmly.

Romi nodded. "We chose each other before we knew people didn't just get to pick their family."

"They do if they want," Madison opined.

"I would have liked to have chosen my family," his mother said with more feeling than she usually showed. "Mine soured me on any familial relationships but mother and son."

"Do you miss them?" Romi asked.

"I do." His mother's face took on a faraway look. "I didn't realize that neither of us was all wrong or all right until *Maxika* was a boy in school and I was too proud to write and tell them where I was."

"So, they don't know?" Romi pressed.

His mother shook her head. "I will never know if my own mama could forgive me and accept the woman I have become. She would have been proud of *Maxika* in any case."

"I'm sure your whole family would admire the man *Little Max* has become." Viktor's tease on Maxwell's other nickname didn't negate his words.

And Maxwell found himself oddly moved by the other man's approval.

"As your family is," Natalya said with a pat to Viktor's hand. "To think you two were once little boys together."

"It's hard to imagine either of them as little anything," Madison said with a laugh.

Romi gave them a droll look. "For me, too."

"I assure you. While he's always had a voice worthy of the little bear I called him, my *Maxika* was a small baby."

"His dad must have been a giant," Romi said with a smile for his diminutive mama.

Large in spirit, at a scant five foot nothing, her stature wasn't nearly as imposing.

"Oh, he was. In so many ways." Natalya winked at Romi.

And Maxwell started wondering again about how soon he could take her home.

"He would be so proud to know how well our son turned out."

"You never said that," Maxwell blurted before thought.

His mother looked more shocked by his blunt admission than he was by her forthright speech.

She reached out to pat his hand. "I never saw the point talking about a man you could never meet."

Maxwell was surprised when not a single person at the table asked why he *couldn't* meet his father.

"I'm sure he would be proud," Madison said.

It was Romi's turn to offer comfort with a caress on his thigh. "I think you got the best of his gene pool anyway."

He grinned down at her. "I am glad you think so."

"Oh, he did. My *Maxika*, he is a son to make any mother proud."

"He's always been a good stick to measure my own success by," Viktor said.

And Maxwell felt the first blush in memory heat his face with uncomfortable prickles. "It has been mutual."

And that was enough admissions for the night. Week. Month. Year. Lifetime maybe. "You wish to host the reception?" he asked Madison.

"Definitely. Have you two chosen accent colors?"

"Blue," he said without hesitation.

"And I bet I know just the shade," Natalya said indulgently as she looked at Romi.

"We could do a metallic pewter with the blue," Madison offered and Romi nodded, looking unaccountably emotional.

Pewter was close enough to black that Maxwell approved the choice. They discussed wedding and reception plans late into the evening.

Maxwell found the domestic scene unexpectedly enjoyable.

Romi couldn't believe how quickly the time leading up to her wedding flew. She, Maddie and the often acerbic Natalya Black went wedding-dress shopping, met with the caterers and tasted more cakes than Romi knew had flavors.

Max was often too busy with work to involve himself in the day-to-day preparations for the wedding. However, he had surprisingly strong opinions on things like whether she wore a veil—he wanted her to wear one—or if there was a ring bearer: Max insisted on one as well as a flower girl.

Romi's oldest cousin's children were going to fulfill the duties. Her grandparents and all her aunts and uncles and their children were coming to the wedding despite the short notice.

Romi was delighted, but sick with nerves at the thought of promising love and fidelity to a man who wasn't making the same lifetime commitment.

She clung to the memory of that one night when he'd said there was no expiration date.

It was easy when he held her at night, or made love to her. During the day while she and Maddie worked on bringing their dreams of a charter school to fruition or the wedding plans, and he was too busy to meet them for lunch or attend yet another cake testing—she hadn't found the right flavor yet—it wasn't so simple.

Her dad was doing well. They'd spoken on the phone again and he sounded so much like the dad of her childhood, she'd cried for an hour after hanging up.

Max had found her and seduced her tears into passion.

She still hadn't brought the blue silk scarves out, but he never mentioned them. There was a little part of her brain that said she'd let him use them after he told her he loved her.

Then she could trust him completely, right?

And she just wasn't sure those blue silk scarves were ever going to see the light of day.

Their sex life was plenty exciting without them anyway. Max wasn't complaining and neither was she.

She had asked him about the fact that Maddie's shares would only revert to her father if Grayson Enterprises was under threat from AIH.

"Jeremy Archer had already begun the initial steps of the takeover. It would have taken some effort on my part, but it could have been manipulated to look like he was the one threatening Grayson Enterprises."

"You're so Machiavellian, it's scary," she said, not sure if she was impressed, or horrified.

Maybe a little bit of both.

"It is a gift." His expression dared her to deny it.

"Some gift," was all she said.

"Grayson Enterprises is already improving."

"With you at the helm, I have no doubt."

"I am not exactly at the helm. I kept on the main management as I agreed to do for your father."

"But you've given them both direction and limits, right?"

"Naturally."

"Being your normal tsar-like self."

"If you say so."

"Oh, I do." She leaned up and kissed him. "I have a strange desire to make love to a tsar. Do you know anyone who might fit the bill?"

He had and the time that followed had left them both replete and winded.

But memory of those blue scarves niggled at the back of her mind, reminding her that he wasn't the only one holding something back in the emotions department.

Maxwell's wedding day dawned bright, the sunshine burning through San Francisco's morning fog.

Romi had spent the night before at her childhood home with Madison Beck.

Viktor had called to complain. "I don't know why I have to spend the night before *your* wedding alone."

"Because we will always give those two whatever they ask." Which did not mean Maxwell loved Romi.

Just that he recognized how necessary her happiness was to his contentment.

Viktor didn't bother denying the truth. "I have to admit I'm surprised you're getting married, Maxwell."

"Yes?"

"Business was always your mistress."

"The same could be said of you."

"Yes, well, as strange as it is to admit, there are things more important than business." Viktor still sounded a little bewildered by that realization.

"I have always known it." Recognition. Respect. These things were as important as his business success.

"I think we're talking different things here."

"You are happy with Madison." Maxwell hadn't made it a question because the truth was there for the most dull-witted to see and he was an astute observer of human nature.

"Happier than I knew it was possible to be." Viktor did not sound embarrassed to admit it, either.

Giving Maxwell the impetus to make his own admission. "Romi fits me and my life perfectly."

"That is good to hear. So, do you have someone to stand up with you?" Viktor asked.

Maxwell had not even considered it. "Do I need someone?"

Viktor made a comment about oblivious bastards.

"I do not suppose it is a task you would care to take on?" Who else would Maxwell ask?

Other than Viktor, he had no friends. Just business contacts and acquaintances.

"I would be honored."

Maxwell breathed out a sigh of relief. "Thank you."

"Romi would have been unhappy if you'd been standing up there alone. She would have felt sorry for you."

"No one ever need pity me."

"Don't I know it? But women see things differently."

Maxwell chuckled. "You are barely married and suddenly you are an expert."

"My grandmother told me."

"Why did Mama not realize this?"

"I don't know, I think your mom is still adjusting to *her Maxika* having another woman at the top of your priorities."

"She is too pragmatic for such sentiment."

"You don't really believe that," Viktor said pityingly.

And Maxwell realized the other man was probably right. "She *wanted* Romi to be sad?"

"Give Natalya the benefit of the doubt. Has she ever even attended a wedding?"

"Not since we emigrated."

"There. She didn't know."

"Isn't it common knowledge?"

"You didn't know."

There was a lot about social niceties Maxwell chose not to learn. If it didn't enhance his business, he wasn't interested.

"Thank you for telling me."

"You are welcome. Just be grateful you don't have to deal with the father-in-law from hell."

"I thought you and Archer were friends."

"We were, until he threatened to commit his daughter. He apologized, but I have random moments when I want to drop him from the windows in his top-floor corner office."

Maxwell laughed. "Romi's father is not mercenary. At all."

"No."

"He's not weak, though." Maxwell had thought at first the man was nothing *but* weakness.

He'd come to appreciate the strength it took to give oneself so completely.

It wasn't in *his* makeup, or at least he'd always believed it wasn't.

"Madison thinks he's Mr. Dad."

"Her and Romi both."

The men shared a silent moment of understanding.

"Just think—you have something to look forward to," Viktor said as they were preparing to hang up.

"What is that?"

"Considering how close Madison and Romi are, we will probably spend most major holidays together."

The idiot was still laughing when the call disconnected. But Maxwell wasn't sure that was such a bad thing. Having a friend rather than friendly rival might actually be worth something.

He was remembering that conversation as he waited in the front of the church for Romi to enter.

A love song popular back in the seventies began to play and then Romi was there on her father's arm.

The older Grayson looked a little rough around the edges, but better despite that. Romi was so beautiful, Maxwell's heart tightened in his chest and it was not a new experience. He still wasn't sure how to handle it though.

She wore a straight gown of pale ivory. It hung straight to the floor with daisy appliqués that were so *her.* She'd worn a veil like he asked, but it was attached to a 1920s-style headpiece.

Romi carried a bouquet of white daises tied together with ribbons of blue and dark gray.

He was sure Madison would insist the color was pewter.

It was only in that moment seeing the two colors entwined symbolically that he realized the gray ribbon was the color of his eyes.

Romi's were shimmering with the love she told him of at least once a day. His favorite was when she called him *my love* while they were having sex.

It always made the experience hotter and more intense for him.

She looked nervous, too. And happy. And so completely focused on him, he actually started forward to join her rather than wait for her to come to him.

The titters that washed through their guests barely registered.

He only stayed in place because Viktor had grabbed his arm. "Don't worry, she's coming to you, *Maxika.*"

Even the diminutive use of his name was not enough to make him turn from the vision of his bride to glare at his best man and only friend.

Romi's smile was blinding as she reached him. She leaned forward and whispered. "A little eager there, *Maxika*?"

Oh, hell. His mother had a lot to answer for. That name was never going to leave him. He just knew it.

"Very eager to make you mine," he replied, making no effort to keep his own voice down.

Even the priest cracked a smile at that.

The wedding went by in a blur. Everything except the promises.

He soaked in every word of Romi's vows, pulling them deep into his soul.

She seemed to be doing the same and when he ended his vows with a "No expiration date," she started to cry.

Thank goodness he got to kiss her then. He hated to see the woman cry. Even if it was in happiness.

Romi danced in Max's arms at their wedding reception.

Madison had gone all out and the ballroom at Parean Hall was decked out in white linen, the fixtures polished to a golden shine, the marble floor pristine. The accent décor and centerpieces were beautiful and every single one of them reminded Romi that she and her gray-eyed man had promised one another fidelity, honor, and to cherish the other. With *no expiration date*.

Her dad looked more peaceful and happy than she could ever remember. He'd even brought Mrs. K to the reception. Romi had invited the housekeeper as a guest, but her dad didn't have to be her escort.

That was all on him and she was proud of him for making the effort.

Jeremy Archer was there, but he was keeping a wide berth of pretty much everyone who mattered in his life.

Romi took pity on him and told her dad to go make nice. They'd been friends for years. Jeremy Archer wasn't perfect, or even nice, but he was a human being and his estrangement with his daughter clearly hurt him.

"You are too softhearted," Maxwell said.

Romi smiled up at him, not worried in the least. "You think?"

"Does he deserve your consideration?"

"Do any of us deserve the second chances we are given?"

Max's smile melted her to her toes. "Perhaps not, *lyubimaya*."

"What does that mean?" He'd never used it with her.

"I will tell you some day."

"But not today?"

He shook his head, the expression in his dark gaze flashing briefly with a vulnerability she could not push against.

She tipped her head back and waited. His kiss came less than a second later.

"Later," she whispered as he pulled his mouth away.

He kissed her a second time and promised against her lips, "Later."

They spent that night glamping, sleeping in a tent at one of the luxury camping resorts that had sprung up around the country. Their accommodations would have made any pasha proud.

In the morning, at the unholy hour of 5:00 a.m., because apparently they had a takeoff slot at six-thirty—though she had no idea where they were going—she asked with a yawn, "So, we spent our wedding night in a tent because why?"

Not that it hadn't been amazing, but even glamping wasn't something she would expect her Corporate Tsar to aspire to.

He smiled enigmatically. "We were practicing for the next two weeks."

"Practicing what?"

But he refused to answer. They spent the private plane ride talking, making love and sleeping cuddled side by side in the leather seats of his private plane.

She started to get a glimpse when the door of the plane opened to reveal the private airfield on Haiti. They joined a group from a worldwide charity that built houses and spent the next two weeks building homes for people who wouldn't have them otherwise.

Watching him pour concrete in a pair of designer jeans and long-sleeved Calvin Klein T-shirt, his head protected from the sun by a San Francisco Giants gimme cap, she realized that even if he never said words of love, and she was starting to suspect *lyubimaya* meant something in that regard, her heart was safe with this man.

And it always would be.

What other man in Max's position would give his new wife a honeymoon that required him to get dirty, sweaty and exhausted every single day and not one of them from really athletic sex?

Okay, so they had their own tent and bodyguards in the one right next to them, but that was hardly the privacy most men dreamt of for their honeymoon.

Not to mention that exhaustion thing. Building a house?

Not for the faint of heart, especially on the schedule they had.

It was neat seeing Max respond to the other members of their group, too. He was the unquestionable leader in any situation, but he took direction when he didn't know how to do something. And he *did not* know how to build a house.

He'd provided the building materials for the house they were working on, though. All of them. Apparently the cargo hold of his plane had been full and he'd had others shipped earlier.

She loved this man and even if he never told her he returned the feelings, she knew he would never walk away from her.

Not after building a house for a family in need to commemorate their wedding.

* * *

Maxwell critically surveyed the sturdy, simple three-room house.

Two small bedrooms, a slightly large living area and tiny bathroom would house a family of three generations and six people. He wanted to add a second story, but the charity coordinators had been clear. They had more houses to build and the family was thrilled. They'd been sharing a smaller space with another family of five.

He had to rethink how much of BIT's profit he donated to charity.

He didn't have to rethink his decision to marry Romi. Any woman who would want to do something so worthwhile for their honeymoon was a keeper.

For life.

And that didn't even scare him a little.

He hadn't said the words, but what others could describe the way he felt about her? The way he just felt happy to be next to her? The way he wanted to make everything better in her life? The way even his own mother stood second to his need to protect Romi's feelings?

He'd called her *lyubimaya* and he was almost ready to tell her what that meant.

CHAPTER THIRTEEN

The bedroom was dappled with afternoon light as Romi lay naked on her and Maxwell's bed. Naked in more ways than one as she waited for her husband to join her for the afternoon tryst she'd set up.

Lying beside her on the bed were the two blue silk scarves.

She'd decided on her honeymoon that the time had come to show Maxwell she trusted him completely.

Footfalls made by Italian leather against hardwood announced his arrival.

"Now that is a beautiful tableau to come home to." He stood in the doorway, his eyes fixed on Romi.

She didn't think he'd even seen the blue silk yet.

She lifted it toward him. "I'm glad to hear you think so."

He stopped in his forward progression as he took in what she held in her hand. His pewter gaze locked on the silk for long, silent seconds before shifting to her face. "Are you sure?"

"Absolutely."

"But I'm still that same guy. The one who blackmailed you into marriage."

"The one who *tried* to blackmail me. You know why I married you Max and it wasn't because of your empty threats."

"They were not empty."

"Are you so sure about that?" she asked, her tone soft

with the love she had no desire to ever hide. "Because I'm not."

"I'm not like your dad."

"Oh, I know." But for the first time, she thought maybe Maxwell wished he could be like Harry Grayson.

"And still you love me."

"And trust you."

He nodded toward the scarves. "Completely. Those say so."

"Yes, they do."

The lovemaking that followed was earth-shattering, but not because he brought her to the pinnacle of pleasure over and over again before allowing her body to complete the journey. And while she learned she absolutely loved being bound by him, that wasn't why, either.

It was the tender way he touched her, the way he treated this like as important a gift as her virginity as her agreeing to marry him. None of which did her Corporate Tsar husband take for granted.

Romi walked into her childhood home, listening for voices.

Max had told her to see him here and she assumed they were having dinner with her dad.

She and Max had been back from their honeymoon for a month.

The charter school was taking shape and Maddie had been thrilled to find out that BIT would be making such a large yearly donation.

It was about half what Max had originally thought because after seeing the way he reacted to the people in need in Haiti, Romi had talked him into donating the rest to projects like the one they'd worked on.

He'd been so moved by the family moving into their new home, Maxwell had insisted on buying them all new bed-

ding and cookware. He'd told them it was his way of hon-
oring the woman who had married him.

Romi had cried. Unashamedly and unreservedly.

It had been an amazing moment.

She walked into the living room startled by the dearth
of furniture. Some pieces still remained, but the sofa and
her dad's favorite leather armchairs were gone. Was he re-
decorating?

Fifteen minutes later, she'd searched the house and found
several rooms in similar states. Her father's study was totally empty, even the bookshelves.

Mrs. K was nowhere to be found and Romi's father
hadn't shown, either.

He'd only been out of the treatment facility for a week,
but he'd gone back to work and showed a passion for his
company he hadn't in longer than she could remember.

"Romi! Where are you, *lyubimaya*?" Max yelled from
the bottom of the stairs.

Her dad would never have done that, but Romi liked her
husband's lack of submission to certain polite behaviors.

She rushed out to let him know she was there. "What's
going on, Max? Is my dad remodeling?"

She would understand if he was. The house hadn't been
changed since Romi's mother died. If Harry were willing to
alter it, that would be a really good sign that he really was
making strides in moving forward with his life.

Maxwell reached for her, even though he wasn't anywhere near enough to complete the intent. When he was
within touching distance, he touched her. All the time.

It was kind of amazing.

His hand dropped by his side. "Not exactly, *lyubimaya*."

"Well, what exactly?" She stood at the top of the stairs,
crossed her arms and tapped her foot.

He waggled his brows at her, showing a playful side he

had just started letting come out. "Come down here and I will tell you."

"You have that look on your face."

"What look is that?" he teased.

Oh, he knew. "Like you're about to make love to me."

"How astute you are."

"Not in my dad's house!" She laughed, though, really pleased that he wanted to, that nothing got in the way of Maxwell's desire to be as near her as he could get.

And most times that meant ultimately joining their bodies.

"Not his house," Max said with a secretive smile. "Not anymore."

"What?" Her dad had sold the house? "Whose house is it?"

"Ours."

"Are you serious?"

"Have I ever lied to you?" he asked, all humor gone.

"No." Not once. She loved this man so much.

He grinned up at her, the playful *Maxika* back. "Now, are you coming down here or am I coming up there?"

"You'd better come up here. There's more furniture." Specifically the bed in her former bedroom.

He took the stairs two at a time and swept her into a truly stellar kiss.

She reveled in his affection, but broke the kiss to ask. "So, you bought me my childhood home?"

Maxwell nodded. "Your dad needs a change."

"Yes."

"So, this is a good house to raise a family."

"I always thought so." Oh, gosh…she was ready to just melt. "Is there anything not perfect about you?"

"How long it has taken to admit I love you?"

"You love me?" She'd hoped, thought…but she couldn't be sure.

"With my soul and the heart I was so sure was dormant."

"You say the cheesiest things."

"But I am sincere."

"And that makes them poetic."

"I should have realized I loved you when I was plotting your downfall and that included you becoming my wife."

"You're used to seeing everything like a business to take over."

"I was scared of what you made me feel, so I hid behind a blackmail attempt. I can't believe you agreed."

"How could I say no? I loved you, too. I love you. So much, Max."

"Yes, well, you are married to a man who is perhaps not as smart as he always assumed."

"Why is that?"

"I wanted a church wedding. That prenup was more a set of strings than arrangements for me to get out of our marriage when I was ready to move on. As if that could ever happen."

"I noticed that." She could be forgiven for a moment of smug reflection.

This man had been worth every risk and she just loved him so much sometimes it hurt how much.

"And the church wedding?" he asked.

She agreed. "A definite sign."

"Did you know?"

"I suspected in Haiti." But she couldn't be sure. Not without the words.

"Because I built you a home to give away."

"Exactly. You're an incredible man, Maxwell Black. My man. My superhero."

"Your tsar maybe."

"Did the tsars love passionately and forever?"

"Some of them."

"Then you are my tsar."

"And you are my wife, the love of my life."

"With no expiration date."

"No."

The kiss that sealed their vows was filled with their love and sparked their passion, exactly how they lived their lives together.

EPILOGUE

Maxwell held tightly to Romi's hand as he followed his mother into the hotel's restaurant.

Inside, waiting to meet him was a group of his family.

Viktor's was there, too.

Like so many things Romi and Madison did, they'd planned this reunion for their husbands with their Russian families.

Two men raised in a new country with a different life here to meet and connect with a heritage they'd never left completely behind.

His mom had been talking to her family for months. All Romi's doing. They were thick as thieves now.

Which was a good thing.

He loved his mother, but he adored his wife.

Her father was with them as well. As moral support, he'd called it.

Harry Grayson had remained sober and started dating his housekeeper two months after getting out of rehab. They were engaged to be married in the fall.

His family still wasn't speaking to him, but they'd made overtures to Romi.

She'd shown something of a ruthless streak herself in refusing anything to do with the rich and powerful Graysons because of the way they treated her father.

Maxwell looked over at where Viktor was hugging a distant cousin, his expression pained, and smiled.

Neither man had gotten any more adept at physical expressions of affection with anyone but their wives. That would change, too, soon.

Because Romi and Madison were doing something else together.

Carrying their first children.

The future stretched out in front of Max in a long winding road that glowed with promise, paved with emotion that might bring pain, but the happiness was worth it.

Very worth it.

* * * * *

If you enjoyed Max's story,
don't miss Viktor's story in
AN HEIRESS FOR HIS EMPIRE
by Lucy Monroe

COMING NEXT MONTH FROM

HARLEQUIN *Presents*®

Available November 18, 2014

#3289 HEIRESS'S DEFIANCE
The Chatsfield
by Lynn Raye Harris

Lucilla Chatsfield has long been the only person to lead her family's dynasty. But when her position is usurped by the intensely arrogant but breathtakingly gorgeous Christos Giatrakos, she refuses to lie low—because Lucilla is playing for keeps!

#3290 TAKEN OVER BY THE BILLIONAIRE
by Miranda Lee

Hotshot entrepreneur Benjamin Da Silva is used to being in the driving seat, but when he finds himself in need of a chauffeur, beautiful, straight-talking Jess Murphy proves that sometimes taking his foot off the pedal can be equally pleasurable....

#3291 CHRISTMAS IN DA CONTI'S BED
by Sharon Kendrick

Billionaire Niccolo Da Conti has everything a man could want, but seeing the unbearably enticing Alannah Collins again has sparked his possessive streak. He'll hire her, seduce her and cross her off his wish list once and for all!

#3292 HIS FOR REVENGE
by Caitlin Crews

Chase is only interested in his dark game of revenge against Zara Elliot's father. What he hadn't counted on? Zara unsettling his rock-hard defences. Losing is never an option for Chase...but winning suddenly takes on a *very* different meaning....

#3293 A RULE WORTH BREAKING
by Maggie Cox

When it comes to work, music producer Jake Sorenson *never* gives in to temptation, but Caitlin Ryan is the ultimate test of his golden rule. As their craving for one another builds to crescendo, they realize that perhaps rules are made to be broken.

#3294 WHAT THE GREEK WANTS MOST
by Maya Blake

Inez longs to escape her father's shadow and follow her own dreams—not be blackmailed into becoming someone's mistress! But it's a thin line between love and hate, and soon Theo unlocks a desire virginal Inez never could have anticipated.

#3295 THE MAGNATE'S MANIFESTO
by Jennifer Hayward

When Jared Stone's manifesto on women ignites global outrage, he swiftly promotes Bailey St. James to calm the storm. Now, with a deal on the line and tensions rising, can it be long before they go from spreadsheets to bedsheets?

#3296 TO CLAIM HIS HEIR BY CHRISTMAS
by Victoria Parker

When Princess Luciana experienced heaven in the arms of her kingdom's greatest enemy, she fled without telling him she was pregnant. Now Prince Thane is determined to secure two very special Christmas gifts—Luciana and his heir!

YOU CAN FIND MORE INFORMATION ON UPCOMING HARLEQUIN® TITLES, FREE EXCERPTS AND MORE AT WWW.HARLEQUIN.COM.

HPCNM1114RB

REQUEST YOUR FREE BOOKS!

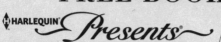 HARLEQUIN *Presents*

 PASSION GUARANTEED SEDUCTION

2 FREE NOVELS PLUS
2 FREE GIFTS!

YES! Please send me 2 FREE Harlequin Presents® novels and my 2 FREE gifts (gifts are worth about $10). After receiving them, if I don't wish to receive any more books, I can return the shipping statement marked "cancel." If I don't cancel, I will receive 6 brand-new novels every month and be billed just $4.30 per book in the U.S. or $4.99 per book in Canada. That's a saving of at least 14% off the cover price! It's quite a bargain! Shipping and handling is just 50¢ per book in the U.S. and 75¢ per book in Canada.* I understand that accepting the 2 free books and gifts places me under no obligation to buy anything. I can always return a shipment and cancel at any time. Even if I never buy another book, the two free books and gifts are mine to keep forever.

106/306 HDN FVRK

Name	(PLEASE PRINT)	
Address		Apt. #
City	State/Prov.	Zip/Postal Code

Signature (if under 18, a parent or guardian must sign)

Mail to the **Harlequin® Reader Service:**
IN U.S.A.: P.O. Box 1867, Buffalo, NY 14240-1867
IN CANADA: P.O. Box 609, Fort Erie, Ontario L2A 5X3

**Are you a current subscriber to Harlequin Presents books
and want to receive the larger-print edition?
Call 1-800-873-8635 or visit www.ReaderService.com.**

* Terms and prices subject to change without notice. Prices do not include applicable taxes. Sales tax applicable in N.Y. Canadian residents will be charged applicable taxes. Offer not valid in Quebec. This offer is limited to one order per household. Not valid for current subscribers to Harlequin Presents books. All orders subject to credit approval. Credit or debit balances in a customer's account(s) may be offset by any other outstanding balance owed by or to the customer. Please allow 4 to 6 weeks for delivery. Offer available while quantities last.

Your Privacy—The Harlequin® Reader Service is committed to protecting your privacy. Our Privacy Policy is available online at www.ReaderService.com or upon request from the Harlequin Reader Service.

We make a portion of our mailing list available to reputable third parties that offer products we believe may interest you. If you prefer that we not exchange your name with third parties, or if you wish to clarify or modify your communication preferences, please visit us at www.ReaderService.com/consumerchoice or write to us at Harlequin Reader Service Preference Service, P.O. Box 9062, Buffalo, NY 14269. Include your complete name and address.

HP13

HARLEQUIN®

Presents®

Rev up for

Miranda Lee's

tantalizing tale of driving desire!

TAKEN OVER BY
THE BILLIONAIRE

December 2014

Jess isn't impressed by Benjamin Da Silva's wealth,
but each glimpse in the rearview mirror has her
aching to climb into the backseat and submit to
his *every* command. She knows she should steer
clear—so why can't she get off the collision course
leading right toward the tempting billionaire?

www.Harlequin.com

HP13296